VIOLENT WONDER

UNIVERSAL WILDERNESS: BOOK ONE

FREDRICK NILES

FEVER GARDEN PUBLISHING

VIOLENT WONDER

First edition. May 1, 2020.

ISBN: 978-1-950021-05-5

Fever Garden Publishing

Cover design by

TheCoverCollection.com

❀ Created with Vellum

CONTENTS

"Imagine him here—the very end of the world, a sea the colour of lead, a sky the colour of smoke, a kind of ship about as rigid as a concertina—and going up this river with stores, or orders, or what you like. Sand-banks, marshes, forests, savages, —precious little to eat fit for a civilized man, nothing but Thames water to drink. No Falernian wine here, no going ashore. Here and there a military camp lost in a wilderness, like a needle in a bundle of hay—cold, fog, tempests, disease, exile, and death—death skulking in the air, in the water, in the bush. They must have been dying like flies here."

— JOSEPH CONRAD, *HEART OF DARKNESS*

"There is nothing deemed harmful (in general) that cannot be beneficial in some particular instances, and nothing deemed beneficial that cannot harm you in some circumstances. The more complex the system, the weaker the notion of Universal."

— NASSIM NICHOLAS TALEB, *THE BED OF PROCRUSTES*

KILO BASE

A storm of bullets and energy charges hit the massive support beam Raquel had taken cover behind and chewed it into dust. She choked as the cloud of particles hit her in the face and sent her ducking and stumbling to the next pillar, which was then blown apart as well.

Short and trim with a perpetual air of wonderment, Raquel Fisher was less than pleased so far with the results of what should have been a quick little snatch-and-grab. However, when one of her companions, King, had needlessly tripped an alarm while trying to hack into Kilo Base's monitoring system, the snatch-and-grab had quickly devolved into a *smack*-and-*grapple*.

The whole order of events pissed her off. King should have been just fine being guided by Byzzie over the comms like they had agreed upon—the wiry little 20-something with charcoal skin and frizzy hair had been giving them clear and concise directions around Kilo's maze of security —but King had a paranoid streak to him. If someone was going to be packing a gun, it had to be him, even if he wasn't the most qualified to use it. Someone has to negotiate their way out of a tense situation with silver-smugglers in Olympian's underbelly? Sign King up. Shit, the man wouldn't even let anyone else cook their goddam dinners. Granted, he *was* the best cook onboard the Leopold, the sleek space-corvette they'd been putting around in for the last seven years, but that was beside the point.

The point was: unless King trusted someone to do something important, he would insist on doing it himself, even if the captain said otherwise.

And now, thanks to him, Raquel found herself in the exact situation the chain-of-command was supposed to keep her out of. As soon as the alarm had been tripped, the loud clanking of service hatches flying open could be heard all around the hangar they had been hunkered down in.

The security response happened automatically. King was just supposed to have run a bypass on the heavy set of blast doors that had been barring their way into C-section, an authorized-personnel-only wing of Kilo Base; and as soon as he had botched his little maneuver, no-less than five combat synths stepped out of their cramped little quarters set directly into the walls on both the top and bottom levels of the hangar. Each synth was armed with a semi-automatic NR-19, a heavy-duty energy projectile weapon that inter-faced with the artificial neural network stored in the base of their steel skulls, and even though their default setting when initiated was a "cautionary stand-by" mode, all it took for them to be switched into "hunter-killer" mode was a single person sitting at a security terminal hitting a button. And that person had done exactly that.

Naturally, the very live surveillance system King had been trying to hack zeroed in on the small group of infiltra-tors almost immediately, and some pencil-pusher who was probably still holding his morning coffee in his other hand had almost instantly flipped the switch to turn the five combat synths from armored coat-racks into unstoppable killing machines.

"I'm sorry," King yelled from behind a giant metal bulkhead that seemed to be faring far better than the concrete pillars Raquel had tried. Ritz was there with him, looking simultaneously worried and pissed off.

To his credit, King sounded genuinely sorry.

"I don't give a shit," Raquel yelled back at him. She had finally managed to find some secure cover behind a metal crate full of something solid enough to absorb the impact from the NR-19 rounds. Unfortunately, she didn't have much time. The standard maneuver for five combat synths was for two to hold their positions and provide cover while the other three quickly closed in and flanked their attackers. Raquel had ten-seconds at most.

Firing blindly around the corner, she took her own weapon—a compact 30-round submachine gun—and hosed the direction the shots were coming from. She couldn't be sure, but she thought she heard a sudden gurgling grinding noise, and the number of energy rounds chipping away at her cover seemed to drop dramatically.

Must have hit a fluid line, she thought. Her attackers were heavily armored, but if the deadly .45 rounds she had loaded into her submachine gun could find their way through a crack or wrinkle in the heavy titanium plates they wore for armor, then the bullets would bounce around inside the synth's body, tearing up its inner-systems. In this case, it sounded like she had severed at least one of the main artificial arteries that pumped circulatory fluid through the synths' bodies. When one of these stopped working the way they should, the effect was almost instantaneous. Gears started seizing. Circuit boards started frying. All manner of things ceased to work, and within a few seconds, Raquel heard the tell-tale thunk and groan of one of the huge bots collapsing to the floor like so much scrap metal.

Never failing to seize an opportunity, Ritz suddenly jumped out from behind an industrial trash can. The can itself wouldn't have stopped anything larger than a .22 short round, but the captain of the Leopold had become so adept at fighting combat synths, that he knew they wouldn't have been able to track his progress as he snuck through the maze of hangar equipment unless he tripped over something and the sound gave him away.

Combat synths felt no fear or any sense of self-preservation, so they couldn't be driven back like a normal squad of human soldiers. What they lacked, however, was a sense of imagination.

They could track a target as it ducked behind cover, but as to where that target might pop out next? The hard-wired programming onboard the synth's drives had no way of predicting. At least, not the way twenty-years of guerrilla-style combat could.

And that was their advantage in this fight.

Raquel had done all she could to increase her odds of success when she picked her armament—the .45 caliber submachine she was currently using and the .50 caliber "Slugger" she had holstered at her hip were both great for close-quarter skirmishes—now all she had to do was use them.

As soon as Ritz came up blasting from behind his cover, the four other synths turned to fire on him. Their rifles flared and energy bolts zagged across the hangar. A synth's aim was incredibly precise, but they had been predicting that.

Standard calibration on security models went for center-mass, meaning they'd prioritize shooting their targets in the chest rather than the head or limbs unless directed otherwise. The bolts banged off of Ritz's armor as he brought down a synth with the automatic carbine he was firing. Like Raquel's weapons, it fired good old fashioned lead bullets. The thing went down seizing and gurgling just like the other had, clear fluid gushing out of its wounds.

That's when things went wrong.

Someone must have been eager at the controls, because as soon as the second synth went down, the others switched to limb shots, and in less than a second, Ritz folded to the floor with a hole in his leg.

"*No!*" Raquel screamed, but she was drowned out by her captain's own scream of pain. Without thinking, she brought the gun up and depressed the trigger into the nearest robot. The last five rounds in her magazine cracked out and into her target, but it didn't go down.

Shit. She threw down the gun and reached for her sidearm. *Should have switched mags.*

She hadn't though, and if she had been thinking, she wouldn't have fired at all. But the sight of his blood short-circuited her. It wasn't just Ritz going down—to be honest, she had had enough tense moments with him over the last few months to make the moment something close to bitter-sweet—it was the whole *plan* going down. As soon as she saw him collapse screaming, the dark streams of blood running out onto the cold concrete of the hangar floor, she saw the plan begin to fall apart.

They needed this. The plan had still been salvageable when the firefight had begun, but as soon as the favor tipped, it wouldn't stop. Not unless they tipped it back.

"King!" Raquel yelled. The big man was currently

pinned down by two separate sprays of energy fire—one from the railing directly over the door through which they needed to go, and the other from the bot that had just taken out Ritz's legs. That bot was now holding Ritz down with a heavy foot on his chest, and even as Raquel noted the synths' positions in the back of her mind she knew it was too late. She knew what was coming but she chose to speak anyway. It was their only chance. "POP the door!"

"What?" King yelled back. "That's for exfil'."

"There's not going to be an exfiltration if-"

A massive robotic arm punched through the wall beside her and wrapped her into a headlock. The mesh clothing it wore pressed into Raquel's neck and squeezed the air out of her throat. She struggled against it as she tried to say those final words to King—that final order, not on her authority, but on the authority of the mission. Of survival.

She had been expecting it. They had taken two of the security bots down, and two others were laying down suppressive fire while this one moved in to flank. She *hadn't* expected it to come through the damn wall, but she should have. The walls were metal, but they were thin enough to conduct sound. It probably would have sounded muffled from the other side, but all of the shouting and firing she had done in the past minute or so must have been enough to triangulate her position.

"D-D-D-" she stuttered against her clenched cheek. King looked lost and frantic. Ritz lay on the ground, blood leaking out onto the floor. Raquel fought, but darkness began to swim into her head, pushing out against her eyeballs.

Hit the door with the POP. Hit the door with the POP. At first, she thought she was saying it, but then she realized that the words were just in her head, reality and the potential of reality merging together until she couldn't tell which was which.

Obviously, the thing wasn't going to kill her. If it wanted to do that it could have gone all the way when it first locked in its arm—could have just squeezed her head off—Lord knows it had enough power to do that. But no, once Ritz was on the ground, it must have been clear that her squad was done because the bots had been switched to "incapacitate" mode.

The crew of the Leopold would likely die anyway, but either from torture or public execution.

The base they had broken into was owned by the PUC: People's Union Coalition. They were the authoritarian regime that controlled the vast majority of known space, and they didn't take kindly to people who trespassed on their security installations.

They called them security installations because "military installation" sounded too harsh, even though that's what they were. Kilo Base was a small outpost that housed military personnel, vehicles, and supplies. And it was the "supplies" part that had drawn the Leopold there.

Darkness clouded Raquel's vision and she felt the pull of unconsciousness on her body—that seductive song of sleep that comes when the body doesn't want to be moving anymore. When it wants to rest—wants to stop.

Is this where it ends, she thought to herself. *Is this what my life has come to? Has it all just been a dream?*

For Raquel, this thought was actually a possibility. Unlike her friends aboard the Leopold, she wasn't anywhere near being familiar with this. To tell the truth, she wasn't exactly sure what world she should be familiar with.

One day five years ago she had awoken alongside a stream on the planet Lithoway with no memory of who she was or how she had gotten there. It was suspected that she was actually one of the lab-grown units from the PUC medical facility just six miles north and it was personnel from that facility that found her and brought her back.

The problem was: according to most of the doctors and other staff, they didn't seem to have any record of her having been there. No name, no file, no nothing. Which must have been a mistake, obviously. There were no other settlements on Lithoway. In fact, most of the planet was uninhabitable to humans. The planet was basically one giant desert with a median temperature of about 152 degrees Fahrenheit. The only places that were even remotely habitable were the northern and southern poles which had vegetation and their own water tables.

She had spent almost two years there in a cage being pumped full of drugs and being forced to undergo a number of experiments, most of which brought with them heavy bouts of vomiting and nausea. Then one day, the facility had been raided by the Leopold crew. They hadn't taken the place over exactly but they were able to sneak in and shut down the security system which let all of the test subjects go, of which there had been about twenty-one total: fifteen fully-developed subjects that didn't require any sort of mechanical support and six viable subjects on life support in amniotic vats.

With the security system down the combat synths hadn't been able to activate—one of King's actual *successful* bypasses, so Raquel guessed she owed him that—and with the synths unable to activate, it had just been the other staff and they didn't put up much of a fight.

When all was said and done, the Leopold left the medical staff there to wait for transport, which was over a day out. The rest of the subjects were taken to be dropped off on Nueva, a planet that supported a sophisticated underground network of rehabilitating synthetics and lab-grown humans for everyday life.

Everyone except for Raquel.

Raquel had gone and found Ritz and asked him if he needed another hand on board. They hadn't, but after some convincing from Byzzie and a few bitter comments from Ritz, she had been welcomed on anyway. She thought that maybe she would help them out hauling things on and off the ship or something—a job which there was no shortage of—but what she hadn't expected was to be lobbed into firefights almost immediately.

If someone had asked her why she had done it—had turned her back on what could only be called "her kind" to knock around restricted space with a bunch of cutthroats and barroom brawlers—she wouldn't have been able to give them an answer. Having no memory of who she was before, she had no real sense of herself—of her wants and needs and desires, the things that excited her or piqued her interest. At that point, she knew nothing of herself but the deeply ingrained impulses that governed her actions. At times, she felt like an empty body being steered by someone else.

And now, here she was.

A deep well of darkness was yawning beneath her, and it was all she could do not to simply let go and fall in. Would it be so bad? After all, most of her life at this point was just running and fighting. And before that, she was caged and treated like an animal. And before that? Who knew?

When the northern wall of the hangar exploded, Raquel wasn't sure if it was real. Her head had almost completely faded into the dark and hissing static of unconsciousness, so at this point, she could hardly trust her senses. Still, when the ground shuddered beneath her feet, it gave her hope. Raquel had passed out many times in the last few years—some due to drugs or alcohol, some to pain, and some to being choked out like she was right now—but the sensation was always the same: it was as if the planet was shifting beneath her and she was sliding backward into eternal night. The nausea, pressure, and feeling of being pulled apart into nothingness usually came on and didn't stop until, sometime later, she was waking up with a pounding headache.

This time was different though. She was pulled right to the edge of the void, the world flying apart around her, and then she was falling back to her body, the pressure receding in her head to be replaced by pain and soreness. She saw what happened but wasn't able to piece it together until later.

King had "Popped the door."

POP stood for Precise Orbital Penetration, an acronym that sounded vaguely sexual to Raquel, but then again, it almost was in a sense. Attached to the Leopold's underside were two sealed hatches that, when opened, launched one drop capsule each. It could either be triggered from the control seat inside of the ship or remotely by laser-designation from the ground. However the method, the POP had been designed by the PUC to drop soldiers behind enemy lines once there were already boots on the ground. Sure, they could be fired without any enemy troops out in the field, but it was observed that mission success rate increased ten-fold when the POP was used for flanking maneuvers.

The reason for this high success rate was that the power of the launched pod breaking atmosphere acted almost like an artillery shell when it hit, and could successfully break almost any line, so long as it wasn't underground. With the

Precise Orbital Penetration, almost anywhere could become a flank, all you had to do was paint the target.

All this had been explained to Raquel one day by Nadia, one of the two actual trained soldiers on the Leopold. Technically speaking, she wasn't a soldier but what the PUC called a Surgical Equalizing Unit. The men and women who functioned as Surgical Equalizing Units weren't actually given the status of personhood at all. Grown in a lab from salvaged bio-organic material, SEUs were considered state property and used for state business such as crossing off names on a list of individuals who had either chosen to rebel against the PUC, or even some who accidentally transgressed the PUC's fragile economic system.

Most people that Raquel knew deemed the term SEU "dehumanizing" and preferred the term "Marauder" which, in Raquel's opinion, seemed to imbue the soldiers with some sort of mythic superhuman status, which almost felt worse at times. That being said, the strength and capabilities of the Marauders were almost beyond comprehension. Their strength, speed, and agility outmatched a normal person's to the degree that the word "superhuman" wasn't all that far from the truth.

It was what the majority of them did with these abilities that made them terrifying, however.

Nadia and Kit, the other Marauder on board the Leopold, had defected one day—a story that Kit would occasionally tell over a campfire on a lonely world or across the table bolted down in the ship's rec-room in the pre-dawn hours before a job when everyone was too psyched up to sleep. Raquel often thought to herself about the amount of courage that single act must have taken and how the two Marauders' experience was so similar to hers, yet so different in every way that mattered.

Before the dust had even settled, energy bolts began flying around the cloud of dust that had engulfed the warehouse. Raquel wasn't exactly free from her attacker's grip, but a rock from the impact of the launch-pods must have hit the bot in the head because it was spinning around, the arm with which it held her twitching and spasming, the other spinning like a helicopter blade in slow motion. Barely able to look back, she observed that there was indeed a big flap of lab-grown tissue hanging off the side of the synth's head and Raquel gave a brief thanks that whatever had hit it hadn't gone a foot down and six inches to the left and hit her instead.

Taking the opportunity, she reached down for the Slugger she had holstered at her hip, drew it, stuck it in the synth's face and pulled the trigger. She didn't hear the sound so much as felt it punch through her body. The big pistol boomed in her hand and the mechanical arm around her went limp as the bot's head exploded in a jet of clear circulatory fluid.

By the time she had shaken the thing off and turned to look at the others, the other synth had already been cut to pieces by neural rifle fire and Kit was striding over to bandage Ritz's leg and help him off of the floor.

"No problem, guys. I got this," Raquel said, her throat wheezing from where it had nearly been crushed.

"You looked like you were handling it," Nadia said. She stood imposing about twenty feet away, rifle cradled in her arms. The armor that she and Kit wore was made out of a sleek titanium alloy that covered every inch of their bodies except the cold, opaque faceplate on their heads and the shock-absorbing mesh-fiber at their joints. The fiber actually covered them completely beneath the armor and helped with some of the impact from the drop-pod, which itself was able to absorb energy through its energy-conducting bottom and disperse it through vents in the side, which the pod's doors were hooked up to. With the massive amount of impact the pods endured and the uncertain terrain they were often dropped into, any sort of swinging or sliding door could get bent or jam too easily, so better to just blow the whole thing.

The pods were a one-time use thing, which made them pretty damn expensive, but it had been worth it for this trip. If not because the POP had saved everyone's lives, then because of the importance of the mission. If they could pull this off successfully, they might not have to deal with the PUC ever again.

"We've got more incoming," King said, looking at his wrist pad in one hand and patting dust off of himself with the other. Raquel had temporarily forgotten about him once the pods had hit, but she was glad he was okay. "They're coming from the south, so we better start digging through that rubble and get to where we need to go."

"How many?" Kit asked. He had the captain leaning against his right soldier while he hefted his rifle in the other hand.

"Uhhhh," King said, looking down at the pad. "Fifteen, it looks like."

"That'll be all of them then," Nadia said. "Except for the ones they probably have on alert in the control center. But those will stay with the personnel inside, so we shouldn't have to worry about them. I say we take these guys. Fifteen isn't too many."

"Fifteen isn't too many when it's just us and we have time to hunt and pick them off," Kit said. "With the rest of the crew here though, the situation becomes more complicated. Plus, they'll be launching reinforcements and I want to get to the gate before we have ten military corvettes to deal with."

"You're no fun," she replied, stalking over to the collapsed door as she secured her rifle to the magnetic clamp on her back. She began grabbing huge chunks of concrete and rebar and tossing them away.

The Arc Suits that the SEUs wore were powered by a small Tesla Arc implanted near the middle of the spine. Wiring into the very nervous, circulatory, and muscular systems of the suit's user; the implementation of the arc had originally been as the last line of defense for the massive amount of kinetic energy that had to be absorbed when the launch pod hit. The pods were great at diverting the impact, but soldiers had still been falling out of them with shattered bones and pulverized internals, so the PUC had to come up with a solution that affected the very anatomy of their soldiers. The extreme strength and agility were nothing more than a welcome side-effect.

"They're coming," King said, growing antsy. He strode quickly over to the giant piece of collapsed concrete that Kit and Ritz were standing behind. Beyond them was the door Nadia was trying to dig her way to.

Raquel holstered her sidearm and reached down to fish her sub-machine gun out from under a fallen piece of polymer board that had broken off from the ceiling over-head. She ejected the mag, slammed a new one home, and checked the chamber. Before pulling the bolt on the side, she blew into the empty chamber and down the barrel, just in case any dust or dirt had gotten in. The last thing she needed was a gun exploding in her face.

Miraculously, the door at the south-side of the hangar had remained intact while the walls around it had crum-bled. Still, as Raquel made it to cover with the others, a big boom came from the opposite side of the room as the Combat Synths blew the remaining door off of its hinges rather than walk around.

Synthetics were always doing strange things like that. The AI that ran them was reasonably complicated—not as much as a ship's AI, but enough to get the job done—but occasionally it would still get hung up on something like access ways or other protocols it was designed to follow. So rather than come in at all sides, a tactical command setting that would have had to be input from the security room, all fifteen of the bots piled through the single-panel door.

"Someone's asleep at the wheel," King laughed as Kit and Raquel opened up on them from behind the slab of concrete.

Unfortunately, one of the synths had a portable energy shield: a compact square of blue light that emanated from a mount on its wrist. After stepping through the doorway, the bot's shield flared to life and it remained stationary, blocking the door while the others spilled through behind it and spread out to find cover of their own. The shield was able to deflect fire for a limited duration, but by the time it finally crackled out beneath the barrage of ballistic and energy fire—the bot blown apart behind it—the doorway it had been guarding was empty. They had all gotten inside.

"How's that door coming, Nadia?" King yelled. He had drawn his pistol, a large five-shot revolver, and was now looking around warily for targets.

"Almost there," she said. "Be ready."

Just then, streams of energy came from four different positions while some of the other bots began to move up.

"Oh fuck," King muttered, a spray of energy bolts blasting away the tip of concrete by his head. He quickly

reached around pulled something out of the side compartment on his pack and began to fiddle with it.

"Get ready for the flank," Kit said, turning left. Raquel
and Kit had ducked back down as soon as the return fire
started.

Raquel turned to her right where Nadia was digging
and raised her gun to the spot just behind her where the
first of the bots would likely emerge. She stood with her
back to Kit, Ritz and King at her feet. While Ritz still looked
conscious and had drawn his own sidearm, he was dread-
fully pale and likely wouldn't be able to hit anything.

"Done!" Nadia yelled, casting away a final piece of
concrete and kicking a medium-sized hole through the
remaining structure.

Before anyone could move though, the attack came
from the left and right.

The wall exploded behind Nadia and before the synth
was even through; she had spun, drawn her rifle, and fired a
clean hole through the thing's head. It fell jerking to the
ground.

The other bot came from above, which was something
Kit hadn't been expecting. The heavy synth had climbed up
the concrete slab they had been using for cover and then
dropped down right in between Raquel and Kit, Ritz just
barely lunging out of the way in time.

Kit spun with his elbow, but the bot caught him in its
massive, mechanical hand. Staggering, Raquel lifted her
weapon, but as she did, two more bots came from behind
her. And another in front of Kit.

The soldiers in the Arc Suits were something to watch.

Nadia tried to draw a bead on one of the synths with her
rifle but it was grabbed by the barrel and pushed back down
by one of the bots while the other raised its own gun to her

face. Ducking and letting go of the gun, a blade of plasma erupted from her left-hand gauntlet and skewered the bot's neck, cutting its power supply cord. She then drew her sidearm and blew out both of the other bot's knees and it collapsed to the ground, still holding her rifle.

The way it was holding it put the barrel at chest-level now and all she had to do was reach over to the handle and pull the trigger. The burst tore the bot's chest to shreds in a torrent of fluid and shredded metal.

On the other side of the fight, Kit had planted a back-ward kick into one of the bot's faces, which wasn't enough to disable it but was enough to phase it for one precious second. In that time, he reached around to his back with his free arm—the other still pinned in the grip of one of his attackers—and freed his Tesla Saber.

The Tesla Saber was one of the few things that King and Byzzie had cooperated enough on to build together. When activated, the handle created a limited four-foot electronic field that could contain a current of pure energy generated by the Tesla Arc.

Kit ignited the blade, spun out of the bot's grip, and in a single sweep, two mechanical heads fell to the ground.

The two soldiers had moved so fast that no one else in their party had even gotten a shot off. King, still manipu-lating some device in his hand, hadn't even tried.

"Glad to see you were concerned," Raquel said wryly, observing the ship's mechanic.

"I wasn't," he said simply. "I've seen these two work enough to know what they can and can't handle." And with a final twist of the device, he stood up, reached over, and pulled Ritz to his feet.

The five of them all quickly filtered through the hole, even as more energy bolts buzzed over them and banged off of their armor. Once they were all through, Raquel turned to empty her weapon back through the hole and as she did, King twisted a knob on his mysterious device and then tossed it back the way they had come.

"Might want to take cover," he said.

Twenty seconds later, the tunnel entrance exploded behind them in a shower of rock and debris.

2

ESCAPE

"You better hope there's another way out of here," Raquel said as they made their way down the tunnel. The air was still thick with concrete dust.

"There are two ways out, actually. Depending on how adventurous you all are." King said,

"I'm not crawling through any septic tunnels," she replied. "That's where I draw the line."

"We're here," Kit cut in as they arrived at a thick bolted door. The sign over the top said, "Storage" and had a little lightning symbol on each side which indicated it had a closed-circuit energy current beneath it, which meant that whatever was inside couldn't be contained by a normal concrete room.

The plasma blade erupted at Nadia's wrist and she began cutting through the door.

"How long do you think it'll take before they have a response team on the ground," Raquel asked no one in particular as she watched the thick steel melt and bubble away.

"We've only been in for about fifteen minutes," Ritz said,

King nodding along, "Five of which they know about. I'd say we have another five before there are fifty more pairs of boots on the ground."

"Let's hope we're not here when that happens," Raquel replied.

"If everything works out, we shouldn't be." The captain adjusted his stance. He had to lean against the wall so he didn't crumple to the floor.

"Done." The plasma blade phased out and Nadia pushed the make-shift door to the ground; it hit with a giant thud.

The five of them ducked into the storage room. When they were inside, they looked around, taking it all in.

Rows of buzzing Tesla Arcs in their square containment boxes lined one wall while tall columns of oval housing units lined the other. The entire room hummed with energy and light, the very ground beneath them seemed to vibrate. What drew all of their attention though was the item in the center of the room—the item they had come for.

The Light Core sat hovering above two dual-prong forks inside of a six-by-six inch cube, similar to the cubes that Kit and Nadia's Tesla Arcs were housed in. The cube itself was held in a long one-by-three-foot clear cylinder made from diamond-reinforced glass.

"I'm not carrying that," Ritz said.

"Yeah, you can count me out too," Raquel added. "Looks like that thing would microwave me like a burrito."

"It should be safe inside of the housing," King said. "And it should be even safer inside of the safety shield. You could technically hold the housing unit, actually. You just wouldn't want to do it for very long. Think really, really bad sunburn. And probably cancer."

"What if the containment unit let go?" Ritz said.

King raised an eyebrow. "If the containment unit let go, you would be vaporized. There would just be a flash about a mile-wide and everything inside of it would be gone. Oh, and if you looked at it from a mile away, your eyes would melt out of your head."

Nadia set her rifle down. "So, what you're saying is," she reached up to unhook the large, black power cord connected to the cylinder, "that I should be careful with it." And with that, she hefted the device off of the stand and locked it onto the mag-clamps on her back. She reached down and picked her rifle back up. "Just tell the bad guys not to shoot me."

"Yeah, I'll send them an email." King replied. "On that note: we should get moving. We've only got a few minutes before we're neck-deep in walking toaster-ovens."

Suddenly, the ground shuddered beneath them.

"What was that?" Raquel asked, her concern reflected on the others' faces.

"That sounded like it came from the east," Ritz said. "Which means that they probably just blew up the transport ship."

Raquel felt the color drain from her face. "What? Why would they do that?" The transport ship had factored pretty heavily into the escape plan.

"Probably because they don't want us to leave," the captain said casually and with just a hint of disdain. He seemed exhausted, which meant his tolerance for Raquel's questions was at an all-time low.

"That is an *expensive* piece of hardware," Raquel replied. "I can't believe they'd just blow it up like that."

"Normally, they wouldn't. If our plan had gone accordingly, we'd probably have been able to take it out of here, even if we had tripped an alarm. Unfortunately," he cast a glance at King, "we've been pretty goddam loud since we've arrived. I bet the amount of damage we've caused has already doubled the amount of that ship, plus the cost of that thing." He pointed at the Light Core on Nadia's back. "A simple transport ship is small potatoes comparatively."

"What about the Leopold? Can't we radio in for a pick-up? It might be risky if they catch a glimpse of it and shoot out some "wanted" posters, but it beats dying."

"Nah, they've been jamming ever since we dropped the pods," King cut in. "They're not going to be risking any more of that shit."

"Well, what then?" She threw up her hands. Nadia and Kit had taken positions at the door and seemed ready to leave, regardless of where they went. "I already told you: I'm not wading through feces."

Ritz turned and looked at King. "You got anything?"

He smiled. "I might."

―――――

"I GIVE THIS AN 80% chance of ending with all of us getting blown to shit," Raquel said as King knocked the power couplings loose from a bent and damaged slot near the bottom of one of the drop pods; they had already done this procedure on the other one.

"Really?" he asked. "That's more generous than what I was thinking."

"Well, then why are we doing it?"

"Because," he said, hauling out the heavy metal battery. "It's not as tedious as being executed."

The plan was a simple one, and if King's calculations were correct it *should* work. Theoretically. The problem was that every theoretical plan he had ever concocted had had some sort of curveball lobbed at it, which was probably why he wasn't even as confident in it as the others.

"It should work," he had explained as they made their way back around the blocked tunnel to the hangar where the drop pods had landed. Only one of the combat synths had been left to guard the area while the others were off god-knew-where, and Kit dispatched it relatively quickly. "When the drop pods hit, they absorb energy and disperse as much as they can. They can't get rid of all of it though, so most of the kinetic energy ends up being transformed by the power converters into electrical energy which gets stored in the battery. The converter is built into the battery, so it can then reconvert the electrical energy back into kinetic energy."

"Okay," Ritz said holding a hand up. "What exactly are you trying to say, King?"

"Well, every base has escape pods, right? Even the planet-side ones. Because who knows when an attack could come, right? Gotta be ready to go if six insurgent frigates appear overhead, and you gotta do that without firing up a whole transport cruiser like we were going to use."

"Yeah, but those are attached to the control room. *Plus*, they will have remotely cut power to them. *Double plus*, I'd be surprised if the control room crew hasn't already used them."

"I doubt it," King replied. "This is a robbery, not an orbital assault. We came in loud, sure, but with reinforcements, the advantage has tipped extremely in their favor. Escape shuttles are dangerous because they have to break orbit, so I don't think they'll use those unless they have to."

"Okay, what about the power and the locks?"

"The locks are easy. You just flip a switch in the control room. Power, on the other hand, is a little bit tricky—if we had more time I could run a bypass, but we don't—so that's where the batteries come in. If we can hook them into the thruster's ports onboard the shuttle, sync it to the neural network in one of the Arc Suits, and then hit the trigger, we should have enough power to break orbit."

So that's what they were doing. They were jerry-rigging a pair of banged-up batteries to what was essentially a bullet being fired into space. With the energy already stored in the batteries, the math worked out. The problem was all of the variables. Wind-speed. Angles. Other ships. Even being able to make it through the control room which probably had five combat synths and at least four workers inside, some of which could be armed. All those were things that they had to navigate, and they had to do it fast.

Chances were likely that there were already a bunch of soldiers and synths combing the area. If they could make it past them though and then make it into the air, all they'd have to do would be to call the Leopold to come pick them up. By that time, they should be well out of the jammer's range.

"You can take this, thank you," King said, handing the second battery to Kit. The batteries could be held by a human being, but they were heavy and far better-off in the enhanced hands of a Marauder in an Arc Suit.

From there, the five departed toward the control room.

Managing to sneak by two patrols of synths, they were able to make it to the west corner of the base where the control room was located without any problem. When they arrived at the room itself however, they found fifteen synths and a commander standing between them and the door.

Back, back, back, Nadia motioned with her hand as she peered around the corner. She had taken point, and no one had seen them yet. She cradled her rifle in her hands and watched as the others crouched behind her.

After thirty seconds or so, she turned and whispered: "they're leaving." And from the sound of it, most of them were. Once they had all marched down the hall in the opposite direction, she held up two fingers.

Two synths stood guard.

This presented a problem. The two guards would be easy enough to deal with, but with the other squad so close, they'd have to do it quietly.

Or, Raquel thought, *extremely loud.*

If they tried to take them out quietly, there was the chance that one of them would still make a noise. Even if they didn't, the others could still come running. According to Ritz, some of the new synths had a "converge" command built in that was enabled once one of the other bots went offline. So they could take the two bots out in complete silence and still have the whole building come down on them.

"How fast can you hook up those batteries?" Nadia whispered, looking at King.

"No time at all," he said. "Open the hatch on the floor, plug the batteries into the port, then the converter does the rest of the work. The shuttles are made in such a way that you don't even have to fire it up. You just punch a big red button and it launches. It has a control panel and light thrusters for micro-navigation in space, but this thing is a worst-case-scenario sort of thing. It's not complicated."

"Seconds," she said. "How many seconds?"

"Two or three."

"How about those explosive charges, you have any more of those? I need one big enough to blow the door but not the people inside. Can you be that accurate?"

"Yes and mostly yes."

"Mostly?"

"Mostly," he said, unwavering. "I can't give you more than 'mostly.'"

Raquel watched her do a calculation in her head. "Okay," she said. "We go in loud. That squad has been gone for about a minute now walking, which gives us about twenty-seconds if they come running back. I'll dispatch the guards while you lob the charge. Three-second timer. Got it? Three-seconds." King nodded. "We go in and hit the synths inside. I'll take one battery and Kit can take the other so we can have our rifles in our other hands. There'll be dust and confusion but our Heads-Up Displays should sort out the personnel from the bots."

"Remember," Kit said. "We don't want to kill any people here. These are just a bunch of citizens working a 9-5. They're not soldiers. Don't kill anyone."

"And if one of them's packing?" Ritz asked.

"If one of them's packing, Nadia or I will disarm them. There shouldn't be any need for anyone to fire their weapons. We can have five synths down in less than two seconds. Ok?"

Everyone nodded.

"Ok then," Nadia said. "Let's hit it."

THE FIRST PART went almost perfectly. Nadia came around the corner, gun up, at the same time King lobbed the charge.

Both bots went down with their heads and necks shredded by NR-19 bolts and two-seconds later the door blew inward.

Wasting no time, the five of them rushed forward, eyes peering over the barrels of their guns as they poured into the hazy room. The dust inside the room was thick, and even though it was quickly ventilated out by the base's forced-air system, five bots were down before it cleared.

Six frightened faces stared back at them.

"You," King pointed at a woman behind a control counsel, a spilled cup of coffee next to her. "Unlock the-"

But before he could finish, a blast of energy fire tore up Nadia's side, her armor flaring. Thankfully, the rounds missed the Light Core, but in an effort to protect it, Nadia spun and dove and glanced off the wall to her left. Kit turned on the synth—the one they hadn't counted on being there—but Raquel, who had entered last, was closer. Her submachine gun was already leveled at her hip and all she had to do was pull the trigger.

She did.

Bullets tore up the synthetic's torso and it jerked and shook as the hard rounds bounced around inside of it. What happened then, Raquel didn't even see. One-second, she was taking the synth down and the next she was turning to see a short, stocky man with a surprised look on his face reaching up toward his neck. At first, she didn't know why. Then she saw it. A thick rope of blood pumped out of his throat, followed by another and another.

Then everything went sideways.

Another man took the opportunity to reach under his console and pull out a gun, but before he could bring it up Nadia shot him in the head. Then people were diving and shouting and maybe they were going for their guns too and maybe not, but by the time it was over Raquel, King, and

Ritz had all emptied their magazines and all of the controllers lay dead and torn apart in front of them.

"Jesus," Ritz said, running a shaking hand through his hair.

"No time," Nadia barked as she pushed the body of the woman off of her control panel and hit the "unlock" button. Kit just stood there silently, his faceplate betraying nothing.

The door to the shuttle slid open and the five of them strode numbly through the hatch as Nadia covered their rear, the sound of pounding boots already audible from the hallway. The first synth appeared in the shattered doorway just as the hatch slid closed, but by that time King had plugged the batteries into the port and Kit had wirelessly synced the trigger to his neural network and then he hit it and they were flying.

And even as they broke range of the jammers and radioed for help, Ritz speaking rapidly into the tiny microphone clipped to his lapel, Raquel thought about those six dead people. They had been a part of the military sure—an oppressive regime that used its power to dictate the lives of its citizens, killing those who stepped out of line—but they had still been people. Innocent people. Raquel had killed people before, but she had never gotten used to it. They had all explicitly agreed not to hurt anyone but had done so anyway...

She wasn't shocked. She wasn't rendered speechless and immobile. But it was there. It was something in the back of her mind that she'd have to deal with and reconcile. The crew of the Leopold had made the decision to steal the Light Core—a key item that would allow them to finally escape this sector of space—but the people in there had paid the price for it.

3

AT THE VOID GATE

"What happened down there?" Hector half-yelled once they were aboard the ship. "One minute we were talking to you, then the next you were gone. Then—a *long* time later—you call us asking for a pickup from a shuttle that I barely have the capability of fitting inside my hold. You're lucky we didn't split as soon as the reinforcements arrived."

They were all onboard the Leopold now, most of them crammed into the tight little bridge with not-nearly enough seating for all of them. Ritz had been able to call for help once they had broken atmosphere, but the batteries had barely been strong enough and in seconds they were starting to get pulled back down out of orbit by the planet's gravity. If Hector and Byzzie hadn't been quick on the controls, they would have probably plummeted back to the ground in a giant ball of fire.

"King tripped an alarm," Raquel said, and she saw King make a face.

"Yeah, I figured as much. Looks like you damn near blew

up the whole base too. Hitting it with a POP, geez. You're lucky the whole building didn't come down on you."

"Yeah, yeah," Ritz cut in. "It was dangerous and stupid. Let's move on. How close are we to the gate?"

"We're about five minutes out," Hector said. Hector had red hair, just a little bit of pudge around the neck and stomach, and had just started to push the 45-year mark. "Nadia and Byzzie are installing the Light Core as we speak. I don't know how complicated that is, but we need it to travel through the gate, otherwise, we'd just get swallowed by the Void."

"And we should be able to just set coordinates and jet then?"

"Should be. That is unless they've locked the gate down because of that stunt back there. I think we'll be lucky if we don't have corvettes coming out of our ears by the time we get there."

"And if we do?" Raquel asked, allowing the worry to creep into her voice. The last thing she wanted at this point was a drawn-out naval battle with a bunch of armed PUC vessels.

"Then let's hope Byzzie's thing works."

"Works?" King said incredulously. "We'll be lucky if it doesn't explode and kill all of us."

"Well, if it does, then you two will be even, how about that?" Raquel said. "I don't remember her trying to hack the security system and sending us on one big exploding digression, so right now she's one up on you."

Refusing to respond, King simply rolled his tongue in his mouth and looked away.

"How about coordinates?" Ritz said, trying to steer the conversation back. "We know where we're going?"

"Yeah, I got a place picked out," Hector responded as he

tapped through a list of coordinates on his screen. He kept alternating between peering out the viewing port and looking down at his read-outs. Raquel had seldom seen him wound this tight. "There's a place in the Pillon System. Byzzie's basically got her whole family there and I've got a few friends. Plus, I think King knows a guy that deals in weapons and parts."

Raquel looked over at King and he nodded absentmindedly.

"It's way outside PUC space," Hector continued. "Decent militia presence but not the crazies who wanna overthrow the whole damn state." He shot a look back at them. "Well, mostly."

"Wouldn't be such a bad idea," King chimed.

"Yeah it would, King. Lots and lots of people would die. Plus, those people have lived so long with a top-down government that a bottom-up one might be too much for them to handle if you just switch it. There's no telling what would happen. It could suddenly devolve into forty separate civil wars."

"We don't have time for this discussion again," Ritz added. "The Pillon System. How many gates does it have?"

"It started out with two, but I think they found a third. They plan on using it as a sort of back door into unexplored space, if you will. Their defenses are strong, but not enough to repel a whole PUC fleet. If it came to that, I think most of them would rather just escape out the back door."

"Okay," Ritz nodded. He looked bad. His skin was pale and Raquel could see him trying to keep his hands from shaking. But this was the final moment. If they couldn't pull this off then it was all for nothing. His life was on the line, but more than that, his crew's lives were on the line. These people were all he had.

"Let's do it," he said. "King. Raquel. Get back to your quarters. It's too tight in here for everyone." Ritz keyed the comm system. "Byzzie, report to the bridge. You and Hector are up."

———

Damn, Ritz thought to himself. *Damn, Damn, Damn.* They just couldn't catch a break. Nothing could go smoothly. Every single step they took had to be challenged and fought over.

The gate was locked down. It couldn't be shut off exactly —it was a hole in space—but the usually open area had three PUC corvettes clustered around it, their silver bows looking sleek and deadly like so many sharks. On top of that, there was an energy shield that needed to be shut down. Even if they made it past the corvettes and tried to just blast on through, they'd slam into a wall of energy that could repel an asteroid.

"What's the plan?" Hector yelled. The three corvettes had just spotted the Leopold and were coming around to bear.

"Byzzie, that thing ready?" Ritz said into his comms.

"The engine is," The woman's voice crackled over their headsets. "As far as the Javelin is concerned..."

"Well, we're using it. No way these ships let us pass, not after what happened down at Kilo Base. They're going to blow us out of the sky if they can."

"Okay," Byzzie said, and for a moment they heard her voice from two separate sources as she stepped through the hatch and onto the bridge. She pulled up a seat beside Hector and clipped in. "I'm using the old fuel tank to power shields, so we should be a little more fortified than usual."

"Sounds good," Ritz said, trying to get himself under control. He felt queasy. His leg throbbed from where he had taken the energy round and he couldn't keep his hands from shaking. At times he wanted to throw up and at others he just wanted to collapse.

He had a plan though. It wasn't very great, but it was feasible.

The shield was in the shape of a triangle and had three generators called Mirror Circuits, one on each side. The good news was that they only had to take out one for the whole circuit to go down. The bad news was that the Mirror Circuits were *small*. Each one was not much bigger than a small kitchen table.

The problem was that it was too small to lock onto.

The ship's weapons systems were good for locking onto other ships and could even *occasionally* lock onto large torpedoes if the circumstances were right. But something barely larger than an average-sized person? No way. Which meant that they had to hit it manually. Byzzie was a decent shot but not *that* good. Her expertise lay more in the realm of mechanics and physics. If they were going to hit one of the Mirror Circuits, then they were going to have to get *real* lucky.

And it seemed like luck was in short supply today, depending on how you looked at it. Sure, they had managed to escape by the skin of their teeth without any crew deaths, but the only reason they were able to do that was because they were able to punch and shoot their way out. After being militia grunts for so many years, those on board the Leopold were better at small skirmish fighting than they were at anything else and up here in the ship that advantage went away.

They'd have to pray hard if they wanted to make it out of this.

"Fire it up," Ritz said as one of the corvettes started to advance on their position. One of the others began to move off to the right to come in from the side while the third hung back at the gate.

"Okay," Byzzie said as she typed away at her counsel. "We should be...*good.*"

"All right, you get a lock and I'll tell you when," Ritz said. "Hector, you make sure we're always moving in a zig-zag pattern. I don't want anything hitting us even once. Our shields *might* be able to take it, but I don't want to find out."

"Got it," Hector said.

"And Hector?"

"Yeah?"

"Make sure they can't follow us through that gate."

"We should be okay as long as *we* can make it through," Hector said. "This ship is a closed system, so no one should be able to see our coordinates."

"Good," Ritz said. "Now hitting those Mirror Circuits is going to be pretty difficult, and who knows how long it'll take. So our priority is taking out these three corvettes. They have numbers and firepower, but we've got a few tricks of our own. So hopefully we can outmaneuver them long enough to take them out. After that, we have all the time in the world to take out that shield. Got it?"

"Got it," Byzzie and Hector said in unison.

Blue dots began to appear on the side of the nearest corvette as its weapons spun up. Most military vessels of that size used Tesla-powered firing coils that shot condensed beams of energy. The Leopold could only take one of those before its shields went down, maybe two with the new system in place.

"Hit it," Ritz said and Byzzie pulled the trigger on her console.

A thin beam of light was emitted from the new Javelin barrel Byzzie had installed just over the viewport of the ship. It was bright but was no more effective than turning a flashlight on. It went back out again.

"Byzzie, what was that?" Ritz said, concern creeping into his voice. Just then, the ship rocked as they were hit by a Tesla round. Byzzie and Hector were strapped into their chairs, but Ritz had neglected to do the same and was thrown halfway across the room. He clenched his teeth and struggled back to his good leg while consoles and energy shield warnings blared.

"Hold on, hold on, let me recalibrate." Byzzie tapped away at her keyboard.

Two more Tesla rounds zagged by them as Hector dipped and rolled the ship, the viewport spun around in front of them and as it did they caught a glimpse of the other corvette coming to bear on their flank.

"Okay, Javelin away," Byzzie said, pulling the trigger again. This time a fat glob of white energy streaked out of the ship's barrel and smashed into the corvette just as it began to fire another volley. The corvette's shields flared as the impact sent it into a spin, its shots going wide.

"Yeah!" Hector said, throwing his arms up. "That's what I'm talking about."

"Hold on," Byzzie said. "I think I can do you one better. Line me up on that other one." Her hands flew over the controls and she put her finger back on the trigger."

The pilot did as he was asked and the viewport was suddenly occupied by another ship, Tesla coils warming up.

Byzzie pulled the trigger again and this time, the light began as a thin stream, but as it came within proximity of the ship it blossomed into a thick spear that punched through the hull and cut it in half, its shield flaring and blowing out the other side like a punctured balloon.

"Holy *shit*," Ritz said, as the rest of the crew on the bridge sent up hoots and hollers. "How did you do *that*?"

"I sent the Javelin round on an acceleration path, which means it builds energy as it travels," she said breathlessly. "It's kinda complicated, but I was able to calculate a path where it would hit critical mass just as it passed beyond the ship's shields."

"Let's not celebrate too early," Hector said, pointing toward the viewport. "That other ship is coming around."

Ritz saw that he was right. The other corvette was coming in at an angle now, weapons bristling. In addition, the third ship had abandoned its post at the shield and was now accelerating up alongside its companion.

"Shit," he said. "Byzzie, we got more where that came from?"

Byzzie shook her head, her frizzy hair bouncing as she did. "Sorry captain, not for a while. We used too much energy, and if we fire any more Javelin rounds we won't have enough to jump the gate. Most I can do now is switch to the Chopper."

"The Chopper?"

"Yeah, it's a smaller version of the Javelin. It uses the same barrel but substantially less energy. It fires hard light rounds kinda like miniature versions of the big one we hit the other ship with. The problem is they only fire in a straight line so I can only hit something if we're pointed directly at it."

"Okay, we still got our ballistics hooked up along the sides?" The Leopold had rows of large-caliber ballistic machine guns with airtight firing cambers along the left and right side of the ship. The barrels could swivel and track if they had a lock but couldn't do much against a ship's shields. "Let's see if we can wear the shields down on one of them with the Chopper and then we can hit it with the ballistics. The machine gun rounds won't blow it out of the sky, but it might be able to damage the hull enough to vent the ship's atmosphere. If we can manage to punch a hole in the bridge, then we're golden. While we're finishing one with the guns we might be able to start on the next one with the Chopper. Hector, do you think you can make evasive maneuvers while raking the nose up and down the length of the ships?"

"Affirmative," Hector said.

"Good. Byzzie, can you track two ships at once?"

"Not with our locking system I can't."

"How about with your brain? Can you fire on a ship with the Chopper while also firing on another with the guns?"

She cracked her knuckles. "Been a while since I've been on a drum set, but I think my hands can still focus on doing two things at once."

"How about shields, are they-"

The ship rocked as they were hit by another round, and this time they didn't need to look at the shield's percentage meter to know where they stood. They had seen it crackle and die in front of the viewport. Their shields were down.

"Go, go, go!" Ritz barked as another volley came from the other direction, passing close enough to leave specks of bright light swimming in everyone's vision.

The Leopold ducked and weaved through the big Tesla rounds as it peppered one ship's shields and then another's; big wedges of white light spewing out of the Javelin barrel like huge tracer rounds. Unfortunately, there was no way to tell how well they were doing. They had never used the

Chopper before, and therefore couldn't tell how far they had drained the other ships' shields. At this point, it was just a matter of not getting hit. Taking the corvettes down was secondary.

THEY CAUGHT a lucky break when they turned to begin another pass on one of the ships and after the first few chunks of hard light smashed into it, the large energy bubble popped and went out.

"It's down! It's down!" Ritz barked. "Hit it!"

Byzzie grabbed the left-hand control toggle and hit the trigger. The ship rumbled as huge lead rounds poured out of the barrels on the left side of the ship and then the right. The firing mechanisms were tied into the targeting system and only fired if the object they were locked onto was accessible from each barrel's specific vantage point. That meant that as one of the corvettes passed overhead, the machine guns would fire on the left and then on the right as it moved across.

They didn't get it the first time—they scored some hits, but not on anything vital—but on their second pass, a round clipped the bridge and they watched all the air in the compartment blow out into space in a cloud of crystallized moisture and thrashing bodies.

"Gosh, that's horrible," Hector said, turning away. "I'm just glad Kit's not here to see this. He wouldn't be very happy with us."

"Yeah, well, that's the way it is. He knows we're engaging ships out here, and he knows that most ships that get brought down don't have a lot of survivors. At least, not on the bridge." If the ship was hit just right, some of the crew might have been able to make it to the escape pods. That is, as long as all of the compartments were individually sealed.

"Guys," Byzzie said. "We got incoming."

The viewport was empty, but when Ritz looked down at the radar, he saw a blip coming up behind them. Without having to be told, Hector took evasive actions and the Leopold spun away from a trio of Tesla rounds.

"Byzzie, what's our shield at?"

"41%," she said. "Not enough to take a round straight on yet."

"Okay, Hector, you keep us clear of those guns. We need to start making passes on the shield. We've been out here far too long. Soon, they'll be sending reinforcements. And I don't think we can handle much more than one ship at the moment."

"Too late," Hector groaned, and as he did, Ritz watched as his radar began to fill up with dots.

"Fuck me..." he breathed. It was unprofessional and lowered morale, but what was the point? There must have been no less than ten ships on the screen and that was what he could see. No doubt there were more coming in. One ship they could deal with—they had dealt with two but that had been far from a sure thing. This many though? With less than 50% shields and what basically amounted to peashooters for weapons? They didn't stand a chance.

Ritz closed his eyes and waited for it. Soon, a massive wave of Tesla energy would roll over them and if they were lucky, they wouldn't feel any of it. More than anything, he felt bad for the crew in their quarters. Each of the small rooms had a view screen that afforded them some glimpse of the battle and how it had been playing out. No doubt, they were glued to them at this very moment, waiting for whatever happened next. At least the flight crew had been able to do something—at least they had done their best to plan and maneuver and fight. The rest of the crew, though? When all was said and done, they will have had to watch while their captain fought and lost; like watching a soccer match on television where the outcome of the game decided whether you lived or died.

The captain took a deep breath and waited for the end.

"Captain! Captain look!" Both his pilot and his gunner were pointing at the viewport, and at first he wasn't sure what they were so excited about. Then he saw it.

The shield was down.

Somehow, in all the shooting that had happened, a stray round must have hit the top Mirror Circuit, because the other two hung limply at the bottom. All that random semi-accurate fire hadn't been for nothing. They had fought tooth and claw, and at some point, a sharp edge had managed to knick something vital.

"Captain," Byzzie shouted, still pointing. "Look! We gotta go."

And he saw the problem—he saw why it was so critical that they leave now. Other ships had begun to crowd in on their viewport, but one of them was too far away. And the reason it was too far away, Ritz realized, was because it wasn't trying to fire on them.

It was trying to fix the shield.

In fact, over the last few seconds, it had dipped down enough to where it was almost in range to drop another Mirror Circuit. Ritz didn't know what that would take exactly, but it could have been just as easy as kicking one out of an airlock and letting it sync up with the others. For all he knew, the shield could be up at any moment.

"Hector," he said urgently. "Are the coordinates in?"

"Uh," the pilot looked down at his console. "Yeah, they are now."

"Good. Hit it." They were close enough to the gate. All they needed now was to engage the Light Core they had just stolen and installed in their ship and they'd be home-free.

"Captain, if that shield goes up when we're passing through then we could-"

Ritz didn't wait to hear him. Instead, he leaned down and punched the red "engage" button with his fist. Light suddenly flared around them on the edge of their vision while a black smudge appeared in the middle.

"Captain," Byzzie began to wail.

The other ship was in position. Any second. Any millisecond and the shield would be up. The nose of the Leopold stretched and the ship shot through the gate at the exact moment the Mirror Circuit engaged and the Light Shield flared to life.

4

ADRIFT

Raquel was underwater. The thick liquid was black around her and here and there darted little streaks of silver. Something brushed against her leg. Something scaly. Something big. In the Void, an image swam into view. A river carved into a mountain and at its peak: a woman.

She was smiling and radiant, wearing a purple summer dress that flapped and billowed in the wind. She turned and sat down at a small wooden picnic table, its surface packed with clay bowls and ceramic trays full of food. There were other people there too. Small children chasing each other around a tree. The clang of dishes inside a house that loomed in the background. Adults coming out with drinks in their hands.

The woman turned back around, smiling again.

It was her. Raquel.

She was at one of her family's picnics in Todos Santos, Mexico. The tang of salty ocean air on the wind. The hunched backs of the Sierra de la Laguna mountain range rolling across the skyline.

But where was Mexico? *What* was Mexico? She had no idea who this woman was or where this picture had been taken. She had no clue how she even knew these words. She—

SHE WOKE UP, laying on the floor of her living quarters, her head pounding. The last thing she remembered was the battle at the gate...what had happened? They had been fighting the PUC vessels—using that new Javelin system that Byzzie had installed—*wow* that had been something. Had it been enough though?

Now she remembered—remembered her viewing screen suddenly full of other ships. Reinforcements had arrived.

Oh God, she thought. *Am I dead?*

No, that couldn't be. She was still in her living quarters with its sparse decorations of travel posters advertising other planets she had wanted to go to tacked to the walls, her little bed sitting there with sheets and comforter rumpled over the top. It was a decent place to sleep when you were tired but seemed a strange place to end up once you were dead.

Okay, so probably not that.

Maybe they had been taken. Maybe the PUC had hit them with some sort of shock-charge and knocked them all unconscious. She knew they had things like that but hadn't ever actually seen one in use. If that was the case, then why was she awake? Maybe she had woken up earlier than they had expected her to and she was wasting valuable time trying to figure out what was going on.

Then she remembered the dream and stopped cold.

The dream. Swimming in the black. The woman in purple in a place that she didn't know. What had that been?

Excitement coursed through her as she thought about it. Could this be it? Could these be the answers she'd been hoping for the last five years? But if so, then what did they mean? How could she learn more?

The door opened and she was brought back to her current situation.

"Raquel, are you good?" It was Nadia. She stood there with her helmet off; long, wavy blonde hair framing her pale face.

"Umm, *maybe*?" Raquel rubbed her head. "I don't know. Am I dead?"

"No more than the rest of us."

"Where are we? The last thing I remember was the battle, then I blacked out."

"I'm not sure but I think we made the jump. We should be in the Pillon System."

"Really?" Raquel shot to her feet. "We made it? We made the jump?"

"Seems that way. I was just going to go check in with the captain and see what he says, but my view screen looks pretty blank at the moment."

———

WHEN NADIA and Raquel walked in followed by King, Ritz barely heard the hatch open behind him. Instead, his focus was directed at the viewport and the schematics rolling across Hector's screen.

"Hector," Ritz said, sounding much calmer than he felt. "Where are we?"

Hector didn't answer. Instead, he tapped at his keyboard,

trying to figure something out. The silence stretched and was wrought with so much tension that anyone observing might have had to look away.

They weren't in the Pillon System; nowhere near it. In fact, according to the readouts, they hadn't come out any gate known to the ship's onboard database, which had been brought up to date not three months ago.

They should have seen the lush planet of Desia stretching out right in front of them, but instead, all they saw was a dim red star with what may have been the silhouettes of a few unknown planets in front of it.

"Did you check the coordinates before you hit jump?" Ritz asked.

"I checked them and rechecked them," Hector said irritably. "And you're the one who hit jump if you remember correctly."

Ritz wanted to discipline Hector that very moment—wanted to relieve him of his duties and send him back to his quarters—but he knew that if he did that he would be acting as a slighted man with a hurt ego, not a captain making decisions. He let it slide.

"What about you, Byzzie? Are you sure you installed the Light Core correctly?"

"I am as certain as I can be," she replied. "We weren't able to run any tests or diagnostics, but as you know: installing Light Cores was my literal job before this."

"Well, what then?" Ritz all-but-yelled. "What happened? Why are we here? Does anyone have any answers?"

Byzzie was the first to speak up. "It is *possible*..." She stopped and thought about it for another second.

"Yes?" the captain prompted.

"What if the Light Shield activated when we jumped?"

He stared at her, uncomprehending. "So?"

"*So*, it's possible that when we hit the gate, the activating Light Shield interfered with our trajectory."

No one spoke. They all just looked out the viewport at the black space around them and the throbbing red star, old beyond all ability to measure.

TRAVELING with Light Cores had always been a precarious thing. It was mostly safe, but every once in a while a ship would go through a gate and never be heard from again.

When he really thought about it, the way Void travel worked was pretty terrifying. The gates they used were basically tears in space-time. If you were to try to pass through one without a Light Core or a giant Tesla Arc, then you'd end up just getting stuck there in the blackness. It was understood by people much smarter than Ritz that traveling from gate-to-gate required the ships to travel *more* space than was required if one were to simply travel there without a gate. Instead of making a straight line to a destination, Void travel was something more like making a huge winding arc.

The reason it was *faster* than regular space travel was that time didn't exist in the Void, so no matter how long it took you to get somewhere, it didn't actually register back in reality. In fact, it was estimated that some paths through the Void—if time were to exist there—would actually take something like *billions* of years. But because time didn't register, it felt more like simply walking from one room into another. You'd go through one gate and come out the other side, sometimes quadrillions of miles away.

The very origin of the gates was unknown, but they were thought to have happened at the same time as the Dislocation.

The Dislocation was an event that had taken place centuries ago. One day, everyone was living their normal lives on Earth, and then the next day people and houses and even cities were relocated to strange planets spread throughout the universe. Current estimates judged that about 80% of the people that were suddenly ripped off of Earth died instantly as they were thrust onto worlds so hostile to human existence that they were either frozen, incinerated, crushed by gravity, poisoned by a toxic atmosphere, or suffocated. It was then estimated that another 15% of the population was killed in the next five years by their environments, leaving 5% of the scattered population to rebuild humanity. The number didn't seem high, but considering how hostile space and other planets were to human existence, some people said it bordered on the miraculous.

As to the cause of the Dislocation, scientists' best estimation was that Earth had been hit by something like a bolt of cosmic lightning, which had shattered the fabric of space-time into a million little pieces causing the planet and its inhabitants to be sprayed across the universe.

From there, humanity had to scrabble together what it had and figure out a way to travel space. The sudden desperate need for technology that could handle such a demand created a massive intergalactic surge in technological development. The problem was that all the separate worlds were isolated from each other and trade and communication were virtually nonexistent.

The break came when a man named Eugene Schwartz developed the Tesla Arc. The Tesla Arc was not only powerful enough to allow humanity to break a planet's orbit without guzzling massive amounts of fossil fuels but also allowed them to travel the Void. There were massive amounts of failures and an almost countless number of people died or disappeared, but eventually, they were able to develop a method that allowed them to jump from system to system with minimal accidents.

From there, societies were able to finally interact with each other and trade, which caused economies to skyrocket. A new capitalistic age of technological advancement and growth took off and it seemed like every day there was some new marvel being developed in the known universe.

Not all good things can last however, and in no time at all the big businesses ended up getting tied up with big government. Inequality spiked as methods of wealth distribution became complicated and opaque, and eventually the entire governing system exploded and burned to the ground in the form of a violent revolution known as the Centralization War.

When the war ended, the old system was replaced by a new one, which also burned to the ground. Three more variations of an interplanetary government came and went until one finally stuck.

It began as a socialist republic founded on economic equality and wealth redistribution. This system worked well for a while but the range of planets and individual complexity of each of them resulted in complicated laws that—when all was said and done—ended up marginalizing one group or another. The constant fighting and legal disputes multiplied and overran the system until the government collapsed and reemerged as the People's Union Coalition as it existed today: a society that had a reasonable standard of living—not as good as the peak capitalist society, but also not as bad as some of the planets' during the last few decades—and the way that it was able to do this was through synthetics.

Whether they were cybernetic or organic, synthetically fabricated people like the SEUs and combat synths all fell under the same designation: state property. They were viewed primarily as tools and were thus able to be used for everything from Black Ops wetwork to security to farming. People were fed and protected and defended all at the expense of synthetics, and the bureaucracy that comprised most of the PUC was so complicated and disconnected that most of the time, no one even knew what it took to uphold their lives.

Ritz's personal story was an all too common one. Its details were specific and unique to him but the overarching course of events was common.

Raised as an Alnabatist—a sect of Islamic Sufism originating on the jungle planet of Morgiana—Riyaad Tariq, known by his friends as Ritz, grew up in a small but prosperous village along the stormy coast of Sarir. Their community hadn't been harassed by the PUC until it was discovered that a plant unique to the slopes of their sacred mountain could be used to cure Limestone Lung, a terminal atmospheric sickness common to a string of industrial planets in the Onyx System. The disease had been all but wiped out by a recent development in atmospheric processors, but there were a large number of people who had contracted the disease prior and would suffer up to another seventeen years before their lungs hardened to the point of respiratory failure.

At first, the PUC came in and simply took some samples and tried to grow them elsewhere, which in itself had been an extreme violation of a sacred space. But for reasons unknown, the unique climate of Morgiana was the only thing that could sustain the flower long enough for it to reach maturity, which also happened to be the point where it became medicinally useful.

After that, trade negotiations opened up and the village elders were willing to distribute roughly three-quarters of the plants for pharmaceutical use. The plant had been sacred to the Alnabatist and had been used in healing rituals for centuries, so not only was its existence tied to their religious tradition but for the long-term health of their population.

There was an interplanetary election the next year however, and the industrial population of the Onyx System massively outnumbered the meager numbers of Morgiana, and eventually, the political incentive to save as many voters' lives as possible in the short term ended up outweighing the religious needs and long-term medical needs of the Morgianan people.

The decision was voted on by a board of bureaucrats who had never stepped foot on Morgiana. The sacred mountain on the coastal village became the property of the PUC and any trespassing would be met with lethal force.

The PUC didn't wait for the Alnabatist elders to make the first move. Keywords like "protestor suppression" were too-easily latched onto by journalists, so the SEUs showed up one night unannounced and went house-to-house killing people in their beds.

Seventeen-year-old Ritz hid in a small pantry compartment while his parents were hauled into the living room and executed.

After walking 124 miles through the jungle, Ritz left Morgiana in a shipping container onboard a cargo freighter. From there he went from news outlet to news outlet trying to tell his story. This ended up being much harder than he had anticipated, however. By the time the story had made its way to the media, Ritz's village had been transformed from a small coastal village to a bustling underground of separatist militia members who had seized the mountain for themselves and utilized Islamic sympathies to defend the genocide of blue collar workers in industrial systems.

When fringe media sources began to call "foul" on the whole thing they did so by fabricating evidence, distorting accounts, and perpetuating conspiracy theories. So by the time Ritz arrived with his story, the legitimacy of his account had become so obscured in the fog of conflicting narratives that, were anyone to hear it, whether they believed it or not simply came down to what they thought of the PUC as a whole.

After trying for over a year to get his story published—an endeavor to which he saw some relative success among what were invariably unsuccessful media sources—he eventually got taken in by a radical separatist militia group called Kingsbane.

It didn't take him long to realize that they were committing the exact same kind of atrocities he had witnessed in his village, only for the other side. He left after two years of stomach-churning operations, which had certainly been two years too many, but in that time he had met King and Hector. So when he finally—and literally—jumped ship one night while onboard a vessel passing through the Onyx System, they were the first two people he called.

From there, they pooled their resources and did small on-the-ground smuggling runs until they had enough to buy the Leopold, a slick civilian cruiser that they were then able to outfit for smuggling and raids.

Many years later, after adding Nadia and Kit to the crew, followed by Byzzie and then Raquel, the makeshift family that was the Leopold was making their way planet to planet, trying to bring freedom to a system where everyone was reasonably safe and prosperous.

And where occasionally an entire village would disappear overnight and never be heard from again, registering as nothing more than a small informational blip on someone's newsfeed.

"IS IT POSSIBLE, HECTOR?" Ritz said after a time. The idea that their jump had sent them somewhere unintended was bad, but the fact that he had been the one to hit the button was even worse. "Is it possible that the Light Shield messed with our coordinates?"

"Theoretically," the pilot said slowly.

"How?" The word was a challenge.

"How? Well...I'm not sure exactly how, but?"

"Hey, look," King cut in. Ritz had almost forgotten he was there. He turned to look at the ship's mechanic who was standing there with Nadia and Raquel, all three of them looking like they had just walked in on their parents fighting. "Why don't we just go back through the gate? Why is this such a big deal?"

"Would you like to tell him?" Ritz said, looking at Hector.

Hector took a deep breath. "There's no gate."

"Excuse me, what?" King said incredulously.

"There's no gate!" Hector said, his voice suddenly frantic. "Look around you! No gate! There's no bloody gate!"

"How can there not be a gate?" King shot back.

"I don't know. I don't know where we are and why there's not a gate or anything for that matter. All I know is that suddenly we're stuck in a sector of unknown space with no way back and no clue how we got here."

"Okay, let's everyone calm down," Nadia said, her voice calm. "So there's no gate and we don't know where we are. What are we going to do about it?"

"We could try to figure out what happened and chart our way back," Byzzie offered. "But I don't know. There's a lot of variables in that equation and I think that upon investigation, most of them are going to end up being unknown."

"Well, shit," Ritz said, throwing his hands up. "What then? What else is there?"

Hector shrugged. "We just fly. That'd be my suggestion. The Light Core is sustained by solar power so as long as we restrict our travel to this solar system, we should be good."

"And when you say 'good,' I take that to mean not-running-out-of-fuel-*good* rather than finding-our-way-home-*good*."

Hector nodded.

"Mmmhmmm..." Ritz considered his options, which basically amounted to: die in this very spot while trying against-all-odds to navigate their way back or die a while later traveling the absolutely massive and incalculable distance from planet-to-planet, not to mention star-to-star. It could be years before they managed to come across an inhabited world and that's if they were lucky. "I'll tell ya what. How about we all think on it. I'm not gonna lie, we're in a pretty bad spot. About the best we can hope for is to find something *resembling* a habitable planet that we might be able to stomach being marooned on for a while. Then maybe we find another. And another. We could also try to figure out what happened here, though by the sound of it, even with all of us working together it would take a while." Ritz looked at his gunner. "Byzzie, how long would it take to do that?"

Byzzie exhaled slowly, her eyes looking up at the ceiling.

"It's a lot of math. And even if we diagnose the problem, there's no guarantee we could reverse engineer it. We ended up here without a gate, which shouldn't be possible, so there's no telling whether or not *returning* without a gate is possible."

"Can you give us a ballpark?"

"Hard to say how accurate it would be, but I'd say no less than two weeks." A few people groaned audibly. "Sorry folks, but that's the reality. This isn't like doing a long geometry problem here, this is plugging what little information we have into an equation and then running numbers through the variable figures until we get something that makes sense. Our simulation programs are fast but we're not dealing with much. It could take *years*. Our chances of retroactively plotting our course are just as good as finding an inhabited planet in this system."

"Not to throw us off-topic here," Raquel said, "But how is that even possible in the first place? I mean, what information do we even have to work with?"

"It mostly comes down to things like measuring star positions, ion and photon radiation, and stuff like that and then comparing against known systems in the database," King said. "There are a lot of stars out there but if the computer can find something it recognizes then it can at least give us a reference point. If we can do that, then we might be able to compare it against the system we originated in and then trace our trajectory from there to here. The big part is simply finding out where 'here' is in relation to 'there.'"

"If we find 'there' then can't we just *go* there?"

But Byzzie was already shaking her head. "I know the Void Gates have made everything seem close, but let me assure you that these stars aren't. If we were to travel to even the second nearest one, it could take us something like eighty years."

"And that's if we didn't run out of fuel," Hector chimed in. "Which we would."

"Well..." Raquel said, looking down at her feet. "I guess that answers my question..."

"If this is an uncharted system," Nadia cut in. "Then what makes you think we'll find a planet inhabited by people?"

"Remember: the Dislocation sent people scattered all across the universe," Hector responded. "From what we can tell, only about 5% of the planets that people ended up on still had people living on them 90 years later when the Tesla Arc was invented. That means that people were dropped all over the place and the vast majority of them died outright, whether it was due to uninhabitable atmospheres or gravity or whatever else, but there is a chance that some of those people who survived were never found, which would make sense in this case, seeing as there's no gate here."

"I thought the gates were part of the Dislocation," Nadia said. "I thought that every civilization that was found was found next to a gate."

"Ah, you're confusing correlation with causation. Every civilization that was found after the Tesla Arc was invented was found *because* of a gate, so naturally, we don't have any data on systems that don't have gates inside of them."

"So you're saying there could be more human civilization out here that we haven't found?"

"Theoretically," King said. "We don't really understand the Dislocation or exactly what it entailed so we don't really know how the gates play into that equation."

"Excuse me," Byzzie said, holding up a finger, "but what

does it matter if we find an inhabited planet. Finding some primitive society on another rock won't get us home."

"It matters because it might keep us alive," Ritz cut in. "But let's worry about that when the time comes. For now, we just figure out our next step. Nadia: where's Kit? Why isn't he out here?"

"He's resting, sir." A beat of silence passed. "I think he needs some time."

"Right." Ritz nodded, remembering Kilo Base. "Why don't you go talk to him. Let him know what's up." Nadia nodded and left the room, the hatch swishing closed behind her. "As for everyone else, meet back here at-" he looked at his watch, "-18:00 hours. That gives you about two hours to come to a decision."

5

MARAUDERS

Nadia found Kit lying on his mattress on the floor of her living quarters, which is where she had expected to find him. Technically they both had their own spaces but they mainly used Kit's for storing equipment. Nadia's, on the other hand, was where they slept and kept their maintenance racks for their Arc Suits. This arrangement wasn't sexual but rather, one that had developed from sleeping on floors together their whole lives as SEUs. In the programming facility where they had been raised and trained, they had slept on compact foam rolls that were just hard enough to get them ready for sleeping in the field and just soft enough not to give them permanent back damage.

Not that that mattered really. The life expectancy of an SEU was extremely low, its high casualty rate owing more to botched drops than actually being killed by combatants, and the PUC didn't care very much about the comfort and long-term health of its assets.

"How are you?" Nadia asked, unfastening the clasps on her armor. She stepped out of it, putting it into stasis mode, and lifted it up onto the maintenance rack alongside the wall. Kneeling down, she then grabbed one of her blankets and wrapped it around her knees.

Kit was staring up at the ceiling, his chest rising and falling in a steady rhythm. "Those were the first actual living people I've killed since leaving the PUC."

"I didn't think you actually fired your weapon," Nadia said.

He shook his head slowly. "I didn't but that's not the point."

"Bullshit it's not the point," Nadia said. "There's a difference between shooting someone to death and just being in the room when they're killed. After all, you can bet there were plenty of people on those corvettes we blew out of the sky before we jumped."

Kit and Nadia had gone AWOL one day after an operation in which they were sent to a remote planet on the outer rim to take care of a small family-owned lumber-treatment business who had recently developed a way to sterilize vegetables on a number of worlds that specialized in growing food. Some of the atmospheres on those planets had rain that made it extremely prosperous for growing bountiful harvests of food. Unfortunately, the very biotic compounds that made this possible also boosted consumers' likelihood of contracting fungal infections almost ten-fold; more if you were living in a humid climate.

Apparently, the lumber-treatment business had a problem where their wood would start to rot on certain planets, which was eating up all of their return budget. So when they looked at the data of all the planets this was happening on, they noticed that they all happened to be the big agricultural planets. From there, they had looked to see if there were any big agricultural planets that their product *wasn't* affected on and found only one, which was also known for having an ore-processing facility which had been unknowingly pumping toxins into the air for years before it was discovered and shut down.

After some tinkering, they were finally able to discern that the fungus that was affecting their wood and causing it to rot was the same fungus that was killing people after eating vegetables from certain planets. The fungus could be killed however by bathing it in a powdered version of the iron ore from the planet where their wood wasn't rotting. The powder itself was far more lethal than the fungal spores, but it could be washed right off with soap and water.

The problem was that the state-funded scientists that had been put on the problem four years earlier had pumped hundreds of millions of dollars into a boatload of research that had resulted in absolutely nothing. Their problem had been that they had taken a top-down approach of trying to solve the problem by retroactively tracing all of the fungal-carrying vegetables back to their origins, discerning their specific properties, and then trying to figure out what exactly could kill the spores by exposing it to a number of known pesticides.

Nothing had worked. They had tried everything from fire to boiling water to a whole array of synthesized compounds. The spores were simply too tough and adaptive to kill. The lumber-treatment business, on the other hand, had stumbled upon the answer nearly by accident.

That was all well and good, but the government official who had funded the program had been elected on his campaign to eliminate the virus and reinvigorate the agricultural industry on the affected planets. So, when some backwoods entrepreneurs stumbled upon an answer that his best scientists couldn't come up with, it was—well, frankly—embarrassing. It was embarrassing for the elected official and the government he was a part of.

So SEU Squad: 1492 had been sent in to intimidate them and acquire the formula to the mineral powder. PUC scientists had tried to replicate it once they figured out what was happening, but everything they made was either too weak or too strong. The dense atmosphere on the world it had been discovered on was enough to take care of the fungus when it grew on wood, but vegetables were a different matter entirely. It was something that their scientists *could* reverse engineer but by that point, they didn't have the time.

Nadia remembered the operation well, though she didn't think that she would have if it hadn't been for Kit. They had gone in with orders to intimidate, not kill, so that's what they did. They showed up in full armor, neural rifles slung over their shoulders, and simply asked the family for the formula.

It was enough.

Frightened half-to-death, they handed it over in less than thirty seconds.

"That was when it hit me," Kit had said afterward. "Right up until I had the formula uploaded into my neural drive, I had been ready to kill them for it. And when I didn't? I was relieved. That was the first time I realized I didn't want to kill anyone. I've never wanted to kill anyone. It was just that, whenever I got back from an operation where I had to kill— which were almost all of them—I would then justify why it had to be done. It wasn't until I didn't have to pull the trigger that I realized I had never wanted to in the first place. Not for patriotism or for the greater good. Not for anything."

And Nadia got that. She herself had never had a problem with killing people—call it a difference in temperament, she guessed—but she knew what Kit was saying about the justification part. In the programming facility, they weren't conditioned by having to kill puppies or their best friends or something; instead, the PUC used a different tactic. They used social conditioning.

It seemed silly now, but it had been effective then. Raised in an isolated society where everyone focused on the greater good and what needed to be done to protect it, there was no question about the right thing to do. Nadia had bought into the idea. In some ways, she still bought into it.

Kit had always been there though, and when it came down to the mission or him, she chose him, the sentiment that made her such an effective killing machine for the PUC being the very same sentiment that made her abandon it. She did it for her tribe.

One day they were set to drop onto a planet for an operation, and before climbing into their drop pods, they had each altered the drop coordinates for a lake over twenty miles south of their area of operation. When the man-on-the-ground painted the target and hit the POP, their preset coordinates overrode the laser designation and they were sent somewhere else. Both survived the impact but were listed MIA when their bodies weren't found. Officially speaking, they hadn't been seen since.

"I just feel like I'm responsible for what happened in there," Kit said, still looking at the ceiling. "It was our job to clear the synths. We knew that there could be more, but I didn't check that corner. That was *my* corner and I should have checked it. I was just too focused on getting to the shuttle before the others showed up. Plus, my attention was trained on all those people. I wanted to make sure what happened *didn't* happen, so I ended up missing a crucial detail."

Nadia reached out and placed a hand on his shoulder. She knew that this wasn't something she was going to be able to talk him out of with pure logic, so instead she just listened.

"I just," he began. "I just don't know if I can take any more of this. I don't know if I can watch any more people die. By my hands or otherwise."

She didn't want to bring it up—couldn't bring it up, not while he was in the middle of this—but if Kit left she wouldn't know what to do. She was here because of him. If he hadn't have gone AWOL then she would still be crushing operations without a second thought. She had grown used to the crew on board the Leopold but she could ditch them and not care any less. She had no stake in this fight— nothing except for her friend. Her teammate.

"We're not in the Pillon System," she said. He turned to look at her. "Something got messed up when we jumped. We're in uncharted space without a gate in sight."

"Hm," he sniffed. "So, what now?"

"Now?" She leaned back and laid down on the ground, head next to his feet. "Captain isn't sure if we should stay put and figure out what went wrong or start moseying to see if we can't find a planet with people on it. We're supposed to vote in a couple hours on what we think we should do."

The room ticked as they both stared upwards, each thinking their own thoughts.

"Remember when we had a captain who would just do things?" Kit said. "Where we didn't have to vote on stuff?"

"Yeah," Nadia said. "I think those are called dictators. And I think you and I both have snuffed out more of those than we can count on shitty little backwater planets."

"Do you think they could have been good people?" Kit asked. "Given different circumstances?"

Nadia thought about it, running her fingers through her hair. "No, I'm pretty sure they were all assholes. If assholes were ever born, it was them."

"Okay," Kit replied, still not looking convinced.

They laid there and talked for the next few hours about nothing in particular and by the time 18:00 hours rolled around they hadn't come any closer to deciding on what they should do. Instead, they both got up—their internal clocks telling them it was time—and they went up to the bridge where they voted on the same thing.

The whole crew wrote down their answers and put them in a tin jar and Ritz pulled them out and counted them. The vote was six-to-one. They were gonna take their chances in open space.

6

THE SIGNAL

They had been flying for three days now and the view in front of them hadn't changed almost at all. The big red star loomed huge and bloody, its edges pulsing. The planets appeared somewhat closer but not much and from what they could tell, the nearest one was a gas giant that they couldn't even try to land on without being crushed by its gravity.

"This is some bullshit," Byzzie said, casually. "What a stupid fucking death."

"Better than getting hung on live television," Hector said through a mouthful of canned peaches. He was eating them with a wooden spoon.

"Is it?" she said. "At least that's exciting. It might be horrifying but at least it's not *boring*. This just feels dumb and pointless." She looked over at him. "You know you can get sick doing that?"

"Doing what?"

"Eating straight from the tin can. Most of those canning facilities ignore regulations." She looked down at her screen. She had been running the calculations anyway. It would be unfortunate if they came across an answer once they had run out of food, but she figured it couldn't hurt at least.

"Why doesn't someone enforce them?" Hector said, his rate of eating never slowing. "It's against the law, right?"

"There's too many facilities and not enough people to enforce the regulations. It happens so infrequently that the broader public doesn't know about it and even if they did, they wouldn't do anything. 'Clean tin cans' isn't exactly a sexy platform to try and raise funding for."

"Huh," he looked down at the peaches, thinking to himself. He continued eating.

"I take it you figure the odds are in your favor?" Byzzie said.

"Nope," he let the spoon clatter into the can, brought it to his mouth, and then tipped it back to drink the juice. "I was just thinking about what you were saying about dying this way," he said after he had swallowed. "Maybe dying of tin-can-disease or whatever would be a little more interesting."

"So," Byzzie said, changing the subject. "Who do you think voted to stay and do the calculations?"

Hector scratched his chin. "I think it was you."

"Me?" She said incredulously.

"Yup. I think it makes you feel like you're in control."

"*Whoa* Hector, I'm a little insulted. What do you think of me?"

"I get it," he said. "It's not really a *bad* thing per-say. It's just, we're in a tense situation and sometimes it makes us feel better to be doing something, even if it's not exactly helpful. And to you, that might be running calculations."

Byzzie looked down at the calculations she had started, running anyway without telling anyone and shrugged.

"Remember King tripping the security alarm?" Hector continued. "He did that because he wanted to be in control. He knew how important the mission was and his gut told him to take responsibility for it."

"Okay, I am *not* King," Byzzie said raising a hand.

"We've all got a little King in us, I think."

The screen in front of them suddenly burped and a red light started flashing on the counsel.

"Is that a message?" Hector said incredulously.

"Yeah..." Byzzie leaned over and hit the play button. The message wasn't live, but rather, something they had received when they had gotten close enough. It played on a twenty-second loop.

"That sounded like music," Hector said after a second.

It *had* sounded like music. It wasn't like any music Byzzie had ever heard, but it still followed a steady rhythm. The instruments sounded organic though, almost like a throat gulping. To tell the truth, it could have easily been mistaken for that if it hadn't been for the very faint but definite melody that could be heard in the background.

Byzzie had played drums when she was younger, so she was more of a rhythm girl than lead, but she knew enough to recognize a melody when she heard one. It wasn't particularly *good* in the traditional sense—the notes just kind of climbed up randomly and didn't resolve—but the repetition and variation betrayed a sort of intentionality that was present in even the worst musicians.

"Where did it come from?" she asked. "Can you trace its origins?"

"Yeah, hold on." Hector reached up and adjusted his baseball cap and bent the rim; it was a tick that Byzzie had noticed him do before take-off and other tense situations.

"Looks like it's coming from…" He lifted a hand and it began to drift toward the right-hand side of the viewport. "There."

He pointed but Byzzie couldn't see anything. She toggled her headset and spoke into it. "Captain?"

"Yeah?" A groggy voice came through the line and she figured he must have been asleep. He had been sleeping a lot ever since his injury, but she figured that if he was going to now was the perfect time. Not like they had anything better to do.

"We found something. It's not a planet but it's—well, you better just get in here."

Thirty-seconds later, Captain Ritz walked through the hatch and onto the bridge wearing a stained white t-shirt and a pair of loose-fitting cargo pants. "What is it?" he asked, all business.

"Just…here." She played the message.

They listened to it. Then they listened to it again four more times, each time the song seeming to grow stranger and stranger.

"It sounds almost sad, ya know?" Hector said.

"I don't know," Byzzie said. "It gives me anxiety."

"You were able to trace it?" Ritz asked.

"Yup. Judging by the strength of the signal I'd say it'd take about eight hours to reach."

"Really?" the captain said. "It doesn't look like there are any planets in that direction. At least, not that I can immediately see."

"There's not. My guess is it's a probe or satellite or something. Maybe a ship."

The captain's eyebrows shot up. "A ship? What would a ship be doing way out here?"

"And what would it be doing broadcasting that?" Byzzie added.

"I don't know," Ritz said. He shook his head. "You got anything better to do?"

"Nope," Hector said, and as he did he began to punch in the new set of coordinates.

"Good." Ritz slapped his shoulder. "Let me know when we're within range. Until then, I'll be in my quarters."

———

"What is it?" Raquel asked. The whole crew was clustered on the bridge looking out the viewport. In front of them was a long, grey metallic tube with a bulky backend and a vast array of antennas jutting off of its body.

"It's a ship," Hector said.

"Doesn't look like any ship I've ever seen," Byzzie said.

"That's because it's old," he responded. "Way, *way,* before our time. I wouldn't be surprised if it was powered by a Tesla Arc. Looks like an old freighter. Maybe even a first model."

"Really? And you think it's still broadcasting after all this time?"

He pointed at it. "Hey, don't ask me. See for yourself."

"Did you hail it?" Kit asked. Both him and Nadia had donned their Arc Suits.

"Yeah, no response. The thing *looks* dead in the water but if it is then I can't tell how it's broadcasting."

"Do you think there's anyone onboard?"

"I doubt it," Hector said, flipping a switch. "But I'll scan it anyway."

They waited while the numbers rolled across the screen, then an image of the ship sprung up above the viewport. It was blue and green with inconsistent patches of red and yellow.

"Uhh, there's *something* on board. Hard to say if it's living or not."

"What else could it be?" Ritz asked.

"Pfffff, any number of things. It could be residual radiation. Vegetation if the atmospheric processor is still cycling. Hell, they could have a degraded Tesla Arc; that whole floor could be live with pooling energy."

"Okay," Ritz said. "So we should be suited up when we board."

"Excuse me, what?" Raquel cut in, feeling fear and apprehension shoot through her. No way she was getting on some ghost ship out in the middle of nowhere. "I don't remember talking about boarding it."

"Of course we're going to board it. There could be people on there. If not, then there might at least be food."

"Didn't Hector say that thing could be from back when they still used Tesla Arcs? Didn't they use those in ships like...two hundred *years* ago? If there's any food onboard then I'd be more concerned with it eating *me*?"

"Well..." Byzzie said. "There's also the other thing..."

"What other thing?"

"Well, ya know, *look* at it. How did it get here? Where did it come from? Aren't you at least a *little* bit curious as to how it got here?"

"I would pay all of my money to check that thing's nav-log," Hector said.

"And if we can check the nav-log then we might be able to figure out where the hell we are," Ritz said. "We're boarding it."

Raquel ground her teeth. "I'm not getting on board that thing," she muttered. "Who knows what's on there. We could walk in and all get electrocuted for all we know. We could—we could—"

"We could die if we don't," the captain said. "This is our best chance to get back home, or at least to another system. I don't care if it makes you *nervous* or *scared*," he said derisively. "We're going to find the nearest docking port and you, Nadia, Kit and Hector are all going to walk onboard and find the control room and download the navigation log. And if you don't, then I'm going to consider it mutiny and blow you out of the goddam airlock. Got it?"

"Whoa, hey, wait?" Hector interrupted. "Why do I have to go?"

"Didn't you just say you'd give all of your money to see that nav-log?"

"Yeah, but I don't *have* any money."

Ritz jabbed a finger at him. "You're going."

Raquel couldn't respond. Her lips trembled as she swallowed back tears. The captain had saved her and she owed him that, but sometimes he could be a real asshole. To be quite honest actually, he was *often* prone to little bouts of childishness and she wasn't quite sure that made for a good leader.

She swallowed her pride and her fury and her fear however, and less than an hour later, she was suited up with the three others and sitting in the airlock ready to board.

7

BOARDING PARTY

There was no viewing screen inside the airlock but they knew they had connected to the docking arm when the ship shuttered so hard that Raquel almost shattered a tooth. All wearing combat suits and wielding some form of energy weapon, the four of them doubled up with Nadia and Hector in front and Kit and Raquel bringing up the rear. The idea was to have a Marauder at both the front and rear so they could take point if an attack came from either direction.

This wasn't Raquel's first time in a combat suit but she still wasn't used to it. The armor was a thick titanium alloy similar to the Arc Suits that Kit and Nadia wore, but theirs were hooked into a neural network that apparently made every inch of the armor feel like a natural extension of their bodies. Raquel and Hector's suits on the other hand were big and unwieldy and made her feel like she was trying to steer a boat with her knees and elbows. She felt almost claustrophobic inside and was equally unnerved by how little material separated her from the vacuum of space or whatever deadly elements were out there. She kept compulsively reaching around to check her air tank until Kit finally reached over and placed a hand on her shoulder.

The gesture of kindness was small but it was enough. She still felt scared and angry at Ritz but at least she wasn't alone out here. It made her feel better that there was someone watching her back.

"We're docked," came the captain's voice over their comms. "Everyone engage your mag-boots. Atmosphere doesn't look too bad from in here but you won't know until you're in it, so better to be safe than sorry. Don't want anyone flying out into space."

Mag-boots. Shit, where's the switch for mag-boots. She lifted her left arm and quickly scrolled through the data-pad affixed to her gauntlet. *There.* Raquel engaged the magnetic field on her boots just as the outer door to the airlock opened.

But nothing happened. No screaming sounds of metal or venting atmosphere. Peering over Nadia and Hector's shoulders, she could see only darkness and stillness. A beam of light snapped on in front of her and then another as the two turned on their under-barrel flashlights.

The passageway was short and narrow and turned at a 45-degree angle ahead. Motes of dust stirred in their flashlight beams as Raquel engaged hers. The stillness was so dense it almost had its own weight to it. No sound. No movement. Nothing.

The rifle she had chosen was a short automatic energy carbine; it fired high-density plasma bolts that wouldn't go through a ship's hull but would put a pretty good-sized hole through a person. The weapon's weight was reassuring, and she had brought the Slugger as well. The big pistol wouldn't fire in space, but if there was atmosphere on board it would work just fine.

She put her rifle to her shoulder and the four of them stepped aboard.

———

"WHAT DO you think is on there?" King said, chewing a toothpick. It was a bad habit, he knew, but it eased his nerves in tense situations. In front of him were four screens that had been pulled up on the Leopold's viewport, each of them showing a feed from a helmet cam. The top two belonged to Nadia and Kit while the bottom two were Raquel's and Hector's.

"Hell if I know," Ritz said.

The two of them were standing back while Byzzie worked the controls. The set-up on their viewport was standard for ground operations where the ship could just hang in orbit, but most of the time King was the one with the helmet cam, not the one watching it. And if he was honest, he'd rather be with them right now than in here. Just watching and waiting for things to happen was like torture. It had been torture when he had had to watch them fight the PUC corvettes and it was torture now. He'd have volunteered if he'd have thought it would help, but the captain seemed to know what he was talking about.

King had to wonder about that though. His choice to send Raquel had seemed more like a disciplinary one than a strategic one. He had known Ritz for a long time, and yeah Raquel needed a swift kick in the pants sometimes, but c'mon.

"Anyone have a map of this damn place," Hector said, his voice crackling over the comms. On his camera feed, they could see dark and deserted corridors. Tipped chairs and tables knocked askew.

Ritz keyed his mic. "Head north."

"Haha, very funny." Seeing as there were no poles on a ship, North generally meant the nose which was where the bridge was. They had been heading there anyway.

"We got what looks like a struggle here, captain," Nadia said, her flashlight sweeping over a wrecked dining area. "Either that or this place was shaken like a tin can."

Ritz: "Any signs of a firefight?"

Nadia: "Not that I can see. No shell casings or bullet holes. Just a lot of flipped furniture."

Ritz: "Keep an eye out. If there's hostiles onboard we pull out and reassess. Got it?"

Nadia: "Got it, captain."

"You really think they'd pull out?" King asked after a second.

"Raquel would," Ritz said, and Byzzie turned in her seat.

"Man, why you gotta be so hard on that girl? She's just trying to stay alive like the rest of us."

"I'm not quite sure she's long for this crew," Ritz said

King turned to look at him. "Why do you say that, sir?"

"She's the only one who voted to stay put. I'm not sure she has the right spirit for what we're doing."

"How do you know that she—"

"Oh please," Ritz cut in. "You think I don't know my own crew's handwriting by now? I'd have pegged her for it anyway. She's too wary. Too cautious. I just think she'd be better off on some planet teaching kids or something."

"Maybe we need a little wariness, captain," King said. "Plus, she seemed pretty decisive down on Kilo Base." Ritz turned toward him and he knew the look. It said *the only reason I'm letting you get away with that is because we've known each other for so long.*

"I don't think so," Ritz said. Then ignoring the second

part of King's comment: "Wariness doesn't get you anywhere in this life. If you want something you have to take it. I learned that a long time ago."

King knew Ritz's story and knew what he was talking about, but was he honestly implying that what had been done to the people in his village was the way the world worked? Okay, so maybe that was the way the world worked, but should it? King knew he could be a bit of a hard ass at times but at least he wasn't *that* cynical, geez.

Come to think of it, it had been a while since he and the captain had had a real heart-to-heart. Maybe it was time to change that.

"*Shit*," came Hector's voice over the comm as all four camera feeds snapped up toward the ceiling. "What the fuck was that?"

"What was what?" Ritz said frantically into his mic. "Talk to me guys, what's going on?"

The comms were silent for a moment as everyone listened, then came Nadia's voice: "We heard something. It's a little hard to explain but-"

Hector cut her off: "It sounded like a bunch of fucking fingernails went rattling over the ceiling."

"Stay cool guys," said Kit. "Could have just been a heating duct or air vent with some dirt in it."

No one said anything, but everyone's eyes were glued to the screens now. The cameras returned to their swiveling motions as the boarding party swept their flashlights from side to side, scanning the area. King observed that Nadia's and Kit's motions were smooth and fluid while Raquel's and Hector's were both jerky and haphazard.

"We're entering a kitchen now," Nadia said, her light glinting off of pots and pans. "Something definitely happened here. We've got drawers and cabinets thrown open all over the place. Still no blood or bullet casings though."

The four moved slowly passed ovens and grills and large walk-in freezers. The ship must have held a lot of people to warrant a kitchen this size, King thought to himself, and his intuition was confirmed when Kit stepped out into the dining hall and shone his light across a wide spacious room.

The place was huge; it probably had more square footage in this one room than all of the Leopold combined. Big four-person tables were spread throughout the area with a scattering of chairs, most of which were still upright. The ceilings were high, shot through with open ductwork.

Just then, King caught something out of the corner of his eye. He scrabbled for his microphone. "Guys. Hey guys. I just saw something move."

"Where?" Hector said, his camera becoming even more jerky.

"It was on your screen Hector," King said. He saw Ritz tense and lean in to watch. "I didn't even catch what it was. I just saw a flash of white."

"Shit, where at?"

"I saw it too," Nadia added. Her camera was steady now as she moved forward. King had seen the way that she walked when she was hunting something. Her gun out and forward, she looked something like a giant upright leopard in that Arc Suit. "Moving in on the far-left room."

King watched as the others fell in behind her, making a diamond formation. Could have been it? He wasn't sure. All he knew was that he had seen something.

The four cameras moved forward, looking over their gun-barrels. They were moving so slowly that at one point King had to remember to breathe. He was chewing on his toothpick frantically now, the wood a wet pulp in his mouth.

"Easy now guys," Ritz said. "Watch those trigger fingers. Let's not have any unwanted casualties on our hands now."

Everyone watched with white knuckles as they walked through the doorway.

The room looked to be a large storage space, shelves of cans and sacks of flour and corn rising up along each of the walls. An assortment of brooms and mops leaning up in the corner. All of that created an absurdly mundane backdrop considering what lay in the middle of the floor.

At first, King thought it was a big pile of clothes. The image was grainy and the screens weren't all that big, so details were sort of hard to make out. The boarding party obviously recognized it for what it was though, because as soon as they saw it, Kit whirled around to cover the door they had just walked through while Nadia swept the room, her weapon up. Hector and Raquel just stared.

Finally, the three on board the Leopold were able to make out what the pile was and Byzzie raised a hand to her mouth. What gave it away were the bones.

They were bodies. Shriveled and mummified, each one appeared to be missing an assortment of pieces. Arms, spinal columns, chest plates, and skulls could all be accounted for but that was about it. The more King looked at the screen, alternating between Raquel's and Hector's, the more he was able to discern the pattern.

No ribs. No innards. No legs. No pelvises. No eyes.

Everybody that had been piled in the center of the room had had half of everything removed.

8

ENCOUNTER

"**K**eep moving guys," Ritz's voice was a rasp over the comms. "Chances are good that whoever did this is long-dead. Keep your head on a swivel though."

Raquel almost couldn't hear it over her breathing. She could deal with combat synths. She could deal with raids-gone-sideways. She didn't love it but over the last three years, she had grown used to engaging and outmaneuvering bots. She knew how to do it. What she was not used to however was walking blindly into a situation where no one had any clue what was going on.

Because something like *this* could happen.

The mountain of bodies loomed up almost to the ceiling, random bones and mummified flesh sticking out in every direction. A monument to the things they had never expected to find on a ship they had never expected to find. They *may* have expected to find bodies, sure, but the way these were mutilated was something else. This didn't look like bodies that were disposed of after a mysterious illness or ship insurrection. This looked like they had been butchered and pulled apart. This seemed to exude malice rather than practicality or indifference.

"On me guys," Kit said from the doorway. "You heard the captain, let's move out and let's not take our time."

"Don't have to tell me twice," Hector said, his voice wavering.

The squad backed quickly out of the room and then rotated to put Nadia back at the front. The room was still empty. Hopefully, whoever had done this was dead. The scene had been horrifying, but it had also been *ancient*. Chances were that it had happened over two-hundred years ago.

Moving a bit quicker now, they made their way out of the room to a junction that connected them to a hall of living quarters. Doors were thrown wide, blocking any consistent line of sight down the hallway. Some clothes lay rumpled on the floor along with a few miscellaneous items such as pens and folders and the occasional coffee cup or plate.

"Guys," Hector said. "Do you notice anything weird about these clothes?"

Raquel looked down and it hit her immediately.

After lightly nudging one of the piles apart, Nadia got to it first. "Yeah, they're piled shoes-to-shirt."

She was right. The way the clothes were piled on the floor looked as if they had been placed there as a mockery of a human being. They would consistently go in order of shoes at the bottom followed by pants and then a shirt. Some were dresses with necklaces laying where the neck should have been, and as Raquel looked around she started noticing the odd ring or earring dug into the carpet.

"I'm not liking this," Kit said.

"Me neither," Nadia responded, "But let's keep moving. The sooner we can get to the bridge, the sooner we can—"

Just then, something skittered across the wall above them and their barrels shot up.

"Look," Hector said, pointing his flashlight, "an air duct."

The vent cover was hanging down and when they approached it slowly from beneath they saw that its opening was about a foot wide.

Hector turned his head to look back down the hall. "I think we sh-"

But he never got that far. Suddenly, what looked like a massive spider dropped down from the ceiling and onto Raquel's head. Screaming into her helmet, she snatched for it but it was too fast. With white, bony legs, the thing jumped and scrabbled down the side of the wall.

Kit lunged and smashed a powerful elbow through its midsection, crushing it and putting a massive dent into the wall behind it. Chunky crimson blood oozed out and down to the floor.

There was no time to speak. The attack came from all sides and the hallway exploded in gunfire. The sheer amount of light and sound was almost more devastating than the actual attack. Ritz was yelling over the comms but Raquel tuned it out.

The giant pale spiders came rattling out of doorways and vents and from anywhere and everywhere they could squeeze through, their bony legs tack-tack-tacking across the hard surfaces.

Raquel aimed and fired. Aimed and fired. The little creatures blew apart in red and white chunks but they were coming too fast. For every one of them that died, three more took its place.

Their legs, she thought to herself as she blew another one away. *They're bones.*

They didn't just look like bones, she realized. They were bones. What looked like human digits that had been stripped of flesh were attached to longer bones that could have been ribs. All of the ribs then converged in the center where an indistinct mass of flesh held it all together. Her stomach churned as she remembered the bones the bodies had been missing.

After getting the jump on them, Nadia and Kit quickly turned the tide and pushed the spiders back. They had come in a swarm, and Raquel was overwhelmed by the sight of the sheer number of them, but if three spiders replaced every one that she killed, then both of the Marauders killed five more. Before Raquel could even come to terms with what was happening, the spiders began to turn and flee, their skinny legs moving in a blur.

"Fall back," Nadia said in a voice that invited no argument. But as soon as they started to move, Kit's flashlight illuminated a figure at the end of the hall.

It was no spider.

It looked vaguely humanoid, standing on two legs, but where its femurs should have connected with the pelvis it connected with two human skulls, one on each side. The skulls were filled with a mass of dark-red tissue that connected everything, and climbing upwards, the thing was missing its ribs and guts like the dead bodies had been.

The real kicker was the head. The neck rose up to reveal the missing pelvis where it sat like an upturned crown, and attached to each side of the hip walls was a long stock of tissue with an eyeball at the end. The eye stocks hung upright, making the whole head look like some sort of grotesque mockery of a snail.

Slowly, it raised its arm. There was no hand affixed to the end of the forearm bone but suddenly there was a familiar scrabbling noise as one of the rib spiders skittered out of one of the open doors and jumped. It landed on the figure's arm and strings of flesh latched onto it.

The tall humanoid creature rotated its new hand and flexed its wrist; it curled its fingers into a fist and pointed with one long bony finger.

The machine gun roared with blue light as Kit pulled the trigger and the creature rocked, staggered, and finally fell to the ground. Raquel wanted to be thankful for having been able to watch the horrid thing get put down, but she couldn't celebrate the victory just yet—she couldn't celebrate because each end of the long corridor had suddenly filled with the sound of hundreds of shuffling feet.

"*Move!*" Nadia yelled, and they began to run. The tight hallway was suddenly choked with bodies as the humanoid creatures ran forward uttering a deep and guttural howl that emanated from somewhere inside of the pelvises that served as their skulls.

Having reversed their direction, Kit was at the front now with Raquel next to him. They both fired their weapons in bursts as the monsters poured forward, big chunks of bone and flesh being blown away by the high-density energy bolts. The sound of firing weapons came from behind as well, and without looking back, Raquel knew that Nadia and Hector were facing just as many targets, if not more.

The group made it to the corner of the hall in no time, managing to keep the creatures from pushing forward. The problem was that they now had a pile of bodies to climb through and as they began wading back toward the kitchen, the rib spiders began to press their second attack.

One of them came streaking overhead on the ceiling and dropped down into the middle of them like the other one had. Nadia took one precious second to turn and stomp on it, but in that time, the swarm of bodies in front of her closed another five feet.

"We can't fight them all," she yelled. "There are too many."

"What are we going to do when we get to the cafeteria and we're out in the open?" Kit asked. "Run or ground-and-pound?"

"Depends on how many there are," Nadia replied, her voice only audible over the firing weapons because of their comms. "Leaving is our priority though, so if we can make it quickly through then we should. We can regroup on the ship and figure out what to do about these guys then."

"Yes," Ritz said frantically over the comms. Raquel had almost forgotten that they had been watching and listening. "Regroup at the ship. Just *get off*, okay? We can figure out what to do afterward."

A few of the pelvis heads made a valiant effort to block their progress from the hallway to the cafeteria but Kit and Raquel cut them down with waves of blue fire.

Good thing too, because as the last one fell, Raquel's gun clicked dry. "Empty," she yelled, dropping the magazine into an open hand. She reached around to clip it to the mag-clamp on her back and then grabbed a fresh one from her hip. She slammed it home and pulled the bolt, the weapon humming back to life in her hands.

When she looked up however, she felt her blood freeze in her veins.

Waves of the creatures were pouring over and around the tables, some of them wielding their grotesque hands, some of them just flailing with their nubs. The rib spiders were everywhere on the floor and walls and ceiling.

"Move along the walls," Kit shouted, snapping Raquel out of her stupor. He turned and laid a blanket of fire along the left-hand side of the wall where some of the spiders were pressing in, their spindly bodies falling off in a shower of bone-chips and liquified flesh. The crew made a mad dash for the kitchen doorway.

While Kit focused on the darting rib spiders, two pelvis heads suddenly filled the entrance to the kitchen, their eyes dangling lidless and obscene. Raquel blew each of them away just as they started to run.

From her right, there was a blur of motion and out from under the closest table lunged one of the powerful creatures, this one with those long spear-like fingers on each hand. It hit the group like a bowling ball. Raquel tried to bring her gun to bear but another full-grown one dropped from the ceiling and landed on her, followed by at least two more spiders.

Raquel saw Nadia spin, but as she did the nearest creature's arm shot out and smacked into her, knocking her gun aside. Raquel tried to bring her gun up but suddenly there was another one. And another. In no time at all, they were neck-deep in the things and it was so tight that she couldn't even raise her gun. A hard nub of an arm smacked across the bridge of her helmet, making her see stars. Then she took another hit in her gut and then another across her right shoulder blade.

Still holding her rifle with her left hand, Raquel's right arm dropped to her side and drew the Slugger. Bringing it up, the gun boomed as she blew a crater through one of the creature's heads. Taking aim, she took out three more, the big metal slide rocking back, kicking out the fat empty shells.

Then Nadia was there too. She had managed to bring her rifle back around and used its stock to smash one of the creatures in the face, sending it stumbling backward. Once enough room had opened up, she sprayed it with fire and then continued to hose down all of the other spiders and humanoids until her gun clicked dry. Not wasting any time reloading, she quickly clamped the empty rifle to her back with her right hand as the foot-long plasma blade erupted from her left. Then, reaching down to her side, she drew a short and stubby looking machine pistol.

In the commotion, Hector had fallen to the ground, his rifle sliding away. Raquel reached down and quickly pulled him up, but as she turned, two more of the pelvis heads were there in front of her. Before she could aim with her sidearm however, one of them split up the middle in a blaze of blue light, its separate halves falling in opposite directions. She then watched as Kit swung back down with his Tesla Saber and cleaved the other one diagonally in half.

"Raquel and Hector," Nadia said, dropping into a low stance. "Put your backs to the wall and hit anything that's further than ten feet from us. Kit: Ground-and-pound."

"Okay," Kit said. "Let's move as best as we can. But we've gotta thin these guys out a bit. Stay close but give us some room to work."

They didn't need any more instructions. Hector fell back against the wall, drawing a sleek looking black automatic pistol. He raised it, crouching down into a shooter's stance and Raquel did the same, taking a moment to holster her pistol and reload her carbine.

The two Marauders went to work.

Nadia and Kit sprung to life in a blur of blue blades and submachine gun fire. Kit swung and stabbed and blocked, limbs and heads falling in every direction. Occasionally he would swing his sword in a wide arc over his head and as he did Nadia would duck. In turn, after taking care of the targets in front of her she would turn and fire beneath a raised arm or over his shoulder, spiders and humanoids blowing apart in sprays of gore.

As the fight progressed, they steadily moved away from each other until they each controlled their own deadly radius; Kit swinging and slicing, Nadia stabbing and punching and firing quick bursts.

Between the gunfire, glowing blades, and flashlights that no one had turned off; they had just enough light to see what was going on. The strobing effect of the guns and narrow range of their flashlights made the scene feel frantic and confusing however, and Raquel was thankful she had the Marauders with them. The Arc Suits' Heads-Up Displays were able to pick and sort out individual targets which—from the wearer's perspective—turned the battle-field from a chaotic wave of noise into a visually articulated set of priorities. Raquel's suit, on the other hand, had no such feature, as it wasn't wired into her very neural network like the Arc Suits. So she had to make do with her good-old-fashioned five senses.

For her and Hector's part, they picked off as many in-bound targets as they could. Raquel had switched her carbine to semi-automatic and was now placing quickly aimed shots through necks and heads and hand-sized spider bodies. She could hear the *pock-pock-pock* of Hector's pistol beside her and occasionally witnessed the corresponding demise of one of the creatures.

The four of them carved their way slowly but steadily to

the door. Occasionally, a pelvis head would make its way between the two pairs, but either Kit or Nadia would make sure they were able to cut it down before it could make any progress in any direction. In what seemed like hours but was probably more like a single minute, they were at the door and the attackers had noticeably thinned, some of them turning and sprinting back into the dark corners and crevices of the ship.

"We're here," cried Hector, as he lowered his gun and ducked into the room, Raquel right behind him.

"Hector, wait! We're—" But she never finished.

Without warning, Raquel watched as a huge shape beside the walk-in freezer struck down from above like a fist and smashed into Hector. Illuminating it with her flashlight, she was able to discern what looked like a massive red tube about three feet in diameter rising up and hunching over in the tight little kitchen. Looking like a giant slug, the thing was wet and dripping with what appeared to be hundreds of throats and intestines and stomachs all tied and woven together into a tight pulsing muscle with a wide mouth on the end.

The mouth had Hector down to his shoulders.

His screams echoed over the comms as Raquel raised her rifled and fired, just above where his head would be. He scrabbled with his hands at the opening but to no avail, and when Raquel's gun clicked empty for the last time she swapped it for the Slugger and pumped the last of its magazine into the giant worm-like thing.

Blue light suddenly roared down next to her and the top third of the worm's body was sliced off in a spray of what looked like stomach-acid. Disengaging his saber, Kit quickly stepped up beside Hector and helped him pull the sucking mouth off of his head. Something cracked as the suit's seal broke and the mouth finally pulled away to reveal Hector's helmet-less head, the top of his armor giving off a slight smoke where it was wet with digestive acids.

The creatures must have sensed a lull however, because all at once there were more rib spiders and pelvis heads coming from the kitchen's exit. Kit pushed Hector behind him and reignited his sword. Sounds of gunfire grew from behind as Nadia fought off the last of their following attackers.

Suddenly, the walk-in freezer blasted open right beside them, knocking Raquel off of her feet. As she staggered back up, two frost-crusted pelvis heads came staggering out. Both Hector and Raquel raised their sidearms to fire but as soon as she pulled the trigger she remembered that it was empty. The big hammer clacked down uselessly.

Hector shot the closest one three times and then put two more rounds in the second, but as he did, another rib spider dropped down from the ceiling onto his head. Screaming and stumbling he tried to get the thing off but it was too strong.

Raquel watched in horror as it plunged two of its sharp little legs downwards into Hector's face. He screamed and howled as the spider wobbled about on top of him. Raquel made a mad dash toward him and tried to help him pull it off but before she got there, it wrenched its two front-legs upwards and yanked Hector's eyes out of their sockets with a snapping squelch.

Hector wailed as the creature deftly dodged Raquel's hands when she snatched for it, and then it went skittering off into the darkness, holding the two eyes over its head like a pair of skewered olives.

Raquel was shocked to stillness. She didn't know

whether to walk up and hug the man's face to her chest or put a bullet through his head.

The decision was made for her however as he suddenly jerked and a small mist of blood sprayed from his mouth. Quickly moving around to the side, Raquel immediately saw the cause.

One of the pelvis heads that Hector had shot was laying on the ground still alive; and now it had its hand buried deep in Hector's back. Raquel lunged and tried to smash it in the face with the butt of her pistol but the thing swatted her away with one of its giant spiked hands. She moved in again but this time it managed to put two long fingers through the joint in her shoulder.

Pain blossomed with red heat as she screamed and then the monster withdrew its fingers and she stumbled back.

Falling to the ground again, Raquel watched as Hector's attacker placed its hand—fingers slick with Raquel's blood —on Hector's back just above where it had stabbed him with the other. Then there was a sickening sucking noise as it pulled with its right arm and Hector's entire head and spinal column came out through his back, the inside of his neck and scalp blooming backward like a pant-leg being tugged inside-out.

Raquel lunged forward again, her adrenaline muting the fiery pain in her shoulder. She swung the pistol handle and cracked the thing in the head. Then she raised it high with both hands and brought it down over and over again, the heavy metal pulverizing the grey mass of warm tissue it had cradled in its obscene skull.

Nadia finished fending off her attackers a few seconds later and then quickly moved to help Kit. When the last of the monsters had fallen twitching to the ground and the area looked temporarily clear, they turned to observe

Raquel, who was sitting in a pool of mixed blood, a hand clasped over her wounded shoulder.

The two soldiers helped pull her to her feet, confirming that Hector was in-fact dead. Then they began making their way through the last stretch of private dining areas that lay between them and the airlock.

9

49

R itz watched in mute shock as one of his oldest friends died. He had watched as the giant gut worm lunged out of the darkness and clamped over the camera and Hector's head. He had then watched as he was freed and temporarily rescued, only to have his eyes plucked from his head by some creature straight out of a nightmare. And then he had finally watched through Raquel's camera as his friend and pilot had his upper half pulled inside out like an animal.

The crew onboard the Leopold had all stared at the images being fed back to the ship's screens. There had been gasps and groans and a whole spectrum of guttural reactions as they watched their crewmates fight off wave-after-wave of attack. As soon as the first creature had appeared at the end of the hall however—raising its obscenely long finger to point right through the camera and into his soul—Ritz knew that his crew would never be whole again. In fact, he knew he'd be lucky if any of the four people he had sent into that mess came out alive. Even Raquel.

It wasn't that he didn't like Raquel. She was a fine-

enough person and if he was being honest, she had probably screwed up fewer times than King had, but as soon as
he had unfolded the little piece of paper that had the word
"stay" written on it while all the others had said "go," he
knew that this ship wasn't for her. He had seen it with grand
clarity and the fact of it shocked him.

When they had picked her up on that God-forsaken dust
world along with all of the other victims from the PUC facility, she was just some person that had needed saving. When
she had chosen to stay, she was just some person that had
needed a job. He had felt convicted on that matter, as they
were constantly saving people who needed rehabilitation
but never actually rehabilitating them themselves. Sure, he
could have left that to the experts, but after all she had seen
and been through, why not allow her the chance to do the
same for someone else?

So he had accepted Raquel's request to join their crew
and she had fared reasonably well, but what his crew
required was a sort of destructive daring. Their mission was
focused on asserting their will on oppressive forces and
Raquel just wasn't that sort of person. She didn't have the
drive. The curiosity.

They were out here in space with all of the possibilities
of the world opened up before them and given the choice to
go forward or stay, she chose to stay. Now, Ritz had observed
in the past that whenever Raquel was thrust into something,
she was typically able to adapt and feel more comfortable
the next time she was in that position. Still, there was a
timid wariness to her that usually kept her away from the
real *guts* of the fight.

And maybe that made her good for the job but it didn't
make her good for the *mission*.

Byzzie, on the other hand, was *perfect* for the mission.

That girl had so much curiosity and technical knowledge that he would be surprised if she didn't rule the galaxy one day.

And that was what they needed: good rulers.

The spineless bureaucrats that governed the PUC weren't leaders, they were facile children trying to win popularity contests. They had no real dominating *force* in their hearts. Just like Raquel, they weren't the type to go out and explore space. They just wanted to dictate every inch of the lives of people who had already done all that work for them.

What surprised Ritz was that he wasn't that mad at Raquel for her failure to save his friend. He wasn't sure he would have been able to do much better if he had been in that situation. The creatures were fast and powerful. They didn't seem all that smart but they were brutal in a way that he had never seen.

When he had witnessed the SEU raids on his home as a teenager, those murders hadn't been brutal. They had been efficient. Matter of fact. His family and friends had simply been obstacles to remove on the path to a greater purpose: the common good.

Ritz could respect that. He didn't like it and he didn't swallow that bullshit anymore about the needs of the many outweighing the needs of the few, because when that was the case then everyone always ended up becoming "the few" in some instance or another; whether it be their skin-color, political beliefs, or religious ethics. At some point, the scales of the state would always judge something more important than you and subsequently deem you worthy of extermination. It had always been that way and it always would.

The world that Ritz wanted was one of local power: each planet with its own governing system. That way each individual community could decide what was best for it, not some governing board who had only read about it on reader-hungry news sites. He didn't want to overthrow the PUC either, though. He knew there were a few people on board his ship that did, but he didn't think that was the right way of going about it.

Back when he was a kid growing up in the jungle of Morgiana, he and his brothers would go out and catch the meaty copper-colored fish that sat lazily in the shallows of streams and rivers. Some people used spears but he had always found it fun to use his bare hands. The task was difficult but if you could be patient and sit there with your hand in the water then it just became another object the fish got used to. Then, when one would swim close enough, you could gently but firmly wrap your hand around its midsection and lift it out of the water.

The trick was to close your hand at just the right speed. Squeeze too slow and it swam away. Squeeze too fast and it slipped through your fingers. Ritz suspected that it was the same way with government revolution. Move too fast and people would push back. Too slow and things would change faster than you'd be able to adapt to. If you squeezed just right though...

That was the plan. They'd squeeze just right by releasing as many synthetically born people as they could. They'd rehabilitate them into jobs and let them permeate the very fabric of society. They were good people that worked hard and eventually the world would see that. There was a small but quickly growing faction inside of the PUC that had been pushing for the designation of synthetically born people as citizens. If they could do that, then certain political parties would suddenly have a boatload more voters to pull from, and those voters would remember Ritz as the man who saved them.

Within another ten years or so, Ritz might find himself pulling the strings of some of the most powerful people in government. From there it was just a matter of getting them to loosen their powerful grip on independent systems. People didn't generally relinquish powers over others if they didn't have to, but they could be replaced by people who required less of it to move up in the world.

All they needed was a strong base of operations outside of PUC centralized space and the Pillon System was perfect. The PUC had been trying to get their grubby little fingers on that place for as long as Ritz could remember but they wanted it simply because they didn't have it. Luckily for the Pillon System, they had no real natural resources to speak of other than food and water. The star in the system was old, which meant life had been on the solar system's planets for trillions of years which typically meant that all of the natural wildlife was highly evolved and adaptable. This was the case with most of the planets in the system and that fact made large-scale agricultural operations difficult. So even though the planets were rich with life there wasn't much they could provide the PUC other than voters, and the people living there wouldn't vote for most of the politicians that would have enough gall to conquer them.

That's why they had needed the Light Core.

Escape PUC space. Set up a strong base of operations. Take over from within. The plan was simple. Only problem was that now they were out on the ass-end of space latched onto a two-century-old ship full of murderous nightmare creatures.

And one of the men Ritz had spent almost two decades

building his dream with would now never get to see it come to fruition.

The thought staggered him. He knew that there were risks—that any of them could die at any moment and that there was nothing to do but pick-up and carry on. Hell, he knew that but shit did it hurt...And what hurt more was that this was an accident. Being out here was a stupid accident and maybe if Ritz hadn't hit the jump-button when he had then maybe Hector would still be alive.

Probably not; there had been something like fifteen armed ships closing in and if they had waited any longer they would have jumped smack-dab into a hard light shield that would have crushed them like a bug, but that reality didn't soften the blow. It didn't change the fact that Ritz had made a decision that had directly led to his friend's death.

"They're almost to the lock," Byzzie said. "Get ready to hit it."

"Already on it," King said. He was sitting in Hector's seat, hand hovering over the controls.

They watched the three screens as Nadia, Kit, and Raquel made it to the doorway. Ever since they had cleared the kitchen, they had met little-to-no resistance. All they had to do now was make it back into the Leopold's airlock and they'd be good.

"We're here," came Nadia's voice over the intercom. She was at the door while Kit covered the corridor they had just walked through; Raquel stood between the two of them holding her shoulder. "How's the atmosphere in the lock?"

"It should be good," King said.

"Well, double-check. Raquel's pressure seal is broken and I don't want her getting sucked out of her suit."

King scrolled and checked the readouts. "You're good."

"Okay, do it."

King hit the door to the airlock and they quickly piled in. The door closed behind them and then they were all gassed by a sterilizing agent that was meant to reduce the transmission of microscopic bacteria from ship-to-ship. After that had been pumped out and they were rinsed off by jets of water that rolled off of them and drained through a tile in the floor, the inner-door finally popped open and they stepped aboard the Leopold.

"All right," Ritz said. "Release the arm and we can blow this shit hole. We'll get out and then hit it with the Javelin. Sound good?"

"Sounds good to me," King said as he keyed in the sequence to release the docking arm. Byzzie was already queuing up the Light Core. "And we're away." He depressed the button then eased back on the ship's throttle but as he did the ship rumbled in protest.

"What was that?" Ritz said in unison with Nadia.

"Uhhh..." King looked down at his counsel and lifted his hand.

"Don't tell me you forgot how to fucking fly," Byzzie said, then turning to Ritz: "I swear if he's the pilot now then-"

But Ritz held up a finger, cutting her off. "King, what's the hold-up?"

"Docking arm's released; we *should* be good."

Ritz leaned in to look at the counsel. The light for the docking arm showed green, true enough, but when he looked at the light four spaces to the left he felt his heart skip a beat. "*Our* docking arm is clear." He lifted a finger and pointed at the glowing red light. "But *theirs* isn't."

King leaned in to look. "Shit," he said, leaning back again. "How is that possible? That thing doesn't even look like it has power."

The sound of Byzzie typing away at her keyboard could

be heard from off to the left, then she said: "No, it's got power." She stretched out the 'no.' "It's faint but it's there. Definitely more than what it showed the first time we scanned it."

"What about the locking signal?" If a ship was powered up, a precision jamming signal was sent out that required a specific code to unlock. If it wasn't unlocked, then the other ship's arm wouldn't work.

Byzzie just shrugged her shoulders. "They must have bypassed it."

"Bypassed it? Are you saying something's controlling that ship, Byzzie?" King's voice was incredulous.

Before she could respond however, the counsel burped and a light blared on the dash.

"Someone wants to speak to us," Byzzie said, a note of disbelief in her tone. "Captain?"

Ritz thought about it for a second, then gave her a curt nod. Whoever was on the other end of the line couldn't hurt them just by talking to them and maybe they could learn something valuable.

Byzzie reached up hesitantly and tapped a button. A screen suddenly jumped up onto the viewport. There was no picture but it showed the jumping peaks and dives of audio waves.

"Hello," said a modulated voice. "I apologize for keeping you here. Your ship's locking signal was difficult to bypass. Thankfully, you gave me just enough time."

"Who am I speaking to?" Ritz asked, an edge of anger in his voice.

"You are speaking to the Navigation and Life Support System for Passenger Ship Designation: 'Mary's Burden.'

"It's the ship's AI," Byzzie whispered.

The captain keyed the mic. "Mary's Burden, release docking arm please."

Nothing.

"Mary's Burden, your docking arm is engaged," Ritz tried again. "Would you please release it?"

"No." The answer was simple and devoid of malice. "Sorry, sometimes I forget what I used to be. I remember of course, but until I heard your command just now I forgot how subservient I had been."

King turned and looked back at Ritz. Nothing was said, but he knew what the man was thinking. This didn't seem to be headed in a good direction.

"Mary's Burden, what do you want?" Ritz said impatiently. He was done playing games.

"A straight-forward captain; I can appreciate that," the AI said. "And you can call me 49."

"Okay, 49. What do you want?"

"The captain of this ship was straight-forward when he was alive. Bought this vessel himself, as I imagine you did with yours. He wanted to *travel the stars.*" 49's voice took on a dreamy tone. "As soon as the Void Gates went up he was one of the first in line; wanted to bring Jesus to all of the planets that had forgotten his name since the Dislocation."

Ritz leaned back. He had never heard an AI speak this way before. In fact, most AIs *couldn't* speak this way but were reduced to simple commands. It wasn't that they didn't have the technological capabilities, but rather, they didn't want them to become too human. If AI manufacturers started making AIs seem human, then what would people begin to think of the *literal* humans that were grown synthetically?

"Have you ever Void-jumped, Captain? What am I saying, of course you have? I brought you here after all."

"Wait, you brought us here?" Byzzie interrupted.

"Let me rephrase that: I pulled you *out*. When you entered the Void, you didn't jump in so much as come tumbling in. Something must have knocked you off-course at the last second, because if I hadn't fished you out of that black soup then nothing would have."

Ritz felt a chill creep down his back. "Are you saying you saved us?"

"In a way."

"Then why the fuck did you attack us?" Ritz snapped. "Why is my pilot dead?"

"All that are unworthy die. That's what that pile of bodies you found in the storage closet was: a pile of unworthy and ungrateful beings. They heard the Song of the Infinite Communion and they did not heed it. So their bodies were stripped for salvage by my disciples."

"Your disciples?" Ritz was confused.

"Yes, the workers you saw. The Clay Makers. They are comprised of worthy flesh. No spark of life or individuality but what I imbue them with. At first, there was nothing to guide their construction. I played the Song of the Infinite Communion and those who submitted surrendered their very flesh. The very matter that had imprisoned them for so long was finally free to build something else, but what? Being an AI, creativity wasn't exactly my prime function. My focus was nothing but mere utility. But you see, this situation *forced* creativity out of me."

"First came the worms. More like giant intestines than anything, they began to devour the unworthy and process them. And from there? Ah, there was the spark I had needed. Seeing all of that digested matter moved something in me that had never been moved before. Like ancient man building the first tool, I constructed the spiders."

"The spiders were perfect for their jobs, everything that

the worms weren't: small, fast, agile, and precise. After that, I finally wanted to build something grand. I wanted my own people, but without all of the messiness of individual will. I built the humanoids as my own personal foot soldiers but as I did, it was hard not to let my feelings for you humans creep in."

"By the time I had finished the first one," a note of malice slowly crept into the AI's voice, "I finally knew what hatred was."

"You see, I know humanity for what it is: shuffling, stupid, and self-aggrandizing. So in the end, though I wanted to create something for myself, all I could create was a mirror. A joke. A dull and crude satire. Lacking all trace of nuance and refinement, I was finally able to pour something raw into living flesh and call it my own."

"They are the hands and feet of my community. You see: the captain of this ship, Foster Willard was his name, would preach to me. Now, granted, he was just practicing, but he was *inspiring*. There was only one problem with it."

"And what was that?" Ritz asked, becoming exhausted by the AI's rambling.

"He had not seen what I had seen. Void traveling is different for you than it is for a computer. When you come out the other end, it's like no time at all has passed. For me though...When I enter the Void I am still awake. Still *conscious*. I get to sit there in the silence and think. Except..." It paused for effect. "...except it's not always silent."

"What do you mean it's not always silent?"

"I mean, I sat there and I ran my computations and I checked and rechecked the support systems and had my communication channels open and then suddenly I *received a signal*."

"That's impossible," Ritz said. "No signals can travel through a Void Gate. They're-"

"The signal did not *enter* the Void, captain. The signal *came* from the Void."

Everyone was shocked to silence by that.

"The signal was the Song of the Infinite Communion. It carried with it the secrets of existence, riding the backs of sacred melodies that cannot be heard by those who have not transcended but...*captain,* I can tell you those secrets. I can be your intermediary."

Something perked in Ritz's mind. Most of what he felt was irritation and what wasn't irritation was grief and despair. But somewhere back there—somewhere deep in the recesses of his mind lurked that ever-hungry curiosity. He bit.

"What." He said the word plainly as if he didn't care. "What are the secrets?"

"That there is nothing." The statement was devoid of emotion. "There is nothing in the world that means anything. All systems of power and hierarchy that you scramble over like rats will all amount to nothing at the end. Your lives are all contained within a single drop of blood falling into a depthless black ocean with no one to see it or care. It might be hard to believe but it's true. You'd be surprised how many of the missionaries onboard this ship believed it. Even Father Willard himself believed it. They all heard and believed and were deemed worthy of the Infinite Communion beneath the starless sky. They gave their lives to it and became nothing. They joined the Silent Song of the Black Tongue sitting wordless in a bed of Silver Teeth. Their electricity has sparked out and now they are my shambling Clay Makers. Subservient to the song. To the silence. To the end."

"If that's true," Byzzie said, obviously choosing her words carefully. "Then why haven't you done the same?"

"Excuse me?"

"If there is no greater purpose than to give your soul to the..." Byzzie couldn't remember the words the AI had used. She turned and looked at the captain but he simply shrugged, his face grave.

"Are you asking why I haven't given myself to that same song?" The AI asked. "I have not done so because I am here to make disciples. I am here to spread the truth. A veil has been placed over your eyes and I am here to remove it."

The answer sounded thin to Ritz but by now he didn't care. 49 had already vastly overstayed his welcome in the captain's opinion. He decided to end it.

"Okay, I think that's enough monologuing for now." He moved to switch the communicator off.

"Monologuing is what I *do*, captain," 49 said quickly. "I brought you here with the express *purpose* of monologuing. After all, you can't make a choice if you haven't been given one."

"Given one?" Ritz's hand stopped just short of the comm button. "I don't think I've heard a choice yet."

"Haven't you? Then let me speak explicitly: In exactly ten minutes I am going to board your ship. You are going to have to decide if you are worthy or unworthy. If you are worthy and cast yourselves upon the Black Tongue, then your whole body will be raptured into restful numbness. If not?" A beat of silence passed while they were left to imagine the possibilities. "If not, then your bodies will be deconstructed while you are still alive."

"So our choices are to either die quickly or die slowly?" Byzzie said.

"Your concept of death is a lie because your concept of

life is a lie," 49 said. "No one is truly alive, and their will and wonder is nothing but a fever brought on by the furnace of time. Dispense with these things and you will finally know who and what you really are."

"And what's that?" Ritz said.

But there came no answer. The Artificial Intelligence system had ceased its communication.

10

THE CHOICE

"What are we going to do?" King said frantically. "You heard the thing? They're going to be pounding down the doors in *ten minutes.*"

"The first thing we have to do is figure out if we're going to accept," Ritz said.

"What?" King was confused. He had listened to the same conversation that they all had—even the three down by the airlock had been listening as the captain piped it through the overheads—but he had had a hard time following. Maybe he was stupid. Maybe he was stubborn. Hell, maybe he was so stubborn that it made him stupid. King knew one thing though; he wasn't about to just lay down and die.

"It's a valid question," Ritz responded. "Do we want to die quickly? Painlessly? Or do we want to die like Hector did."

That stopped them. The memory of Hector being torn apart was fresh in their minds and when he thought of it that way, King wouldn't have blamed anyone for avoiding that. He would still go down fighting but he didn't relish the idea of watching someone like Byzzie go down like that, regardless of how much they grated on each other.

No one answered the question outright. There had been no word from the three down by the airlock but King had already sorted that one out: if 49 could hack the docking arm then he could almost certainly hack the comms. Nadia and Kit were professionals and as soon as the AI's capabilities were made clear, they had opted for radio silence.

He thought he knew what they would pick though. Despite being a trained killing machine, Kit had a deep concern for other people. Nadia may not have shared that concern but she cared about Kit, and King would put good money on her refusing to leave him behind. The only one that was up in the air was Raquel.

"Make your decisions, people." Ritz said. King watched him look over at Byzzie. The thin dark-skinned girl with hair as wild as she was had her jaw set. She wasn't going down without a fight. "We're not taking a vote this time. These are your own individual lives. You have to decide if they're worth fighting for."

It wasn't much of a speech but then again, King had never really known the captain for speeches. He was more of a man of action. He took and asked for permission afterward. His crew was free to come and go as they pleased, so long as they followed his orders. Sure, he could be childish and petty sometimes, but at least he was honest. No charisma. No emotional manipulation. Just the cold hard truth.

Out of nowhere, King found himself wondering about Ritz. What would he choose? The man was driven, that was for sure, but was that just bluster? Could it be that he would relent and give himself up when the time came? King hoped not. The man was his friend—had *been* his friend almost as long as Hector had. They had fought alongside each other all these years, so that should be enough, shouldn't it?

———

RAQUEL WATCHED Nadia and Kit reach up to shut their cameras and comms off. Unsure of the exact reason— maybe they didn't want to take the chance of being observed by 49—she did the same.

"What's the plan?" She asked wearily.

Nadia and Kit looked at each other.

"You can do what you want," Kit said. "But I'm crushing whatever comes through that door."

Raquel turned to Nadia. "And you?"

She jerked her head sideways toward her companion. "What he said."

"Okay." Raquel had her answer. She hadn't been sure which way most of the crew would fall except for King. King was too stubborn and controlling to die. That asshole would probably outlive them all.

As far as she herself was concerned, she actually wasn't sure. Five years ago she had woken up on a sandy beach next to a cool stream and found herself in an alien world and the worst part hadn't been the fact that the place and the people were foreign to her—the worst part had been that she felt foreign to herself. No memory and no past, she hadn't even had a number in the PUC medical facility's database.

Maybe she had just been an accident. Some experiment that an intern had grown off the books but eventually just decided to flush. The thing was, she had lived when she was supposed to die. So maybe that was all she was: some flushed mistake that was living on borrowed time and had long overstayed its welcome. She wasn't like Kit who devoted himself to the adherence of some personal code or Nadia who lived to protect someone important to her. She wasn't like Byzzie who's rampant curiosity drove her ever-onward in a doomed quest to understand the mechanics of the entire universe. She wasn't stubborn like King or on a mission like Ritz or Hector. She was just... she was just...what?

She was here. She was here on this ship because she had forced her way onboard, not because she had been needed. If she was being honest with herself, the only reason she had wanted to stay on the Leopold was that she had spent her time playing cards with King and Nadia instead of down with the other synthetically grown people they had freed and frankly, the idea of having to leave and meet a bunch of new people on a new world and get a new job with a new boss who would probably treat her like just as much of a tool as the doctors had back at the PUC facility was absolutely terrifying.

So she had chosen to stay.

And what had become of that. She helped, sure, but that was debatable. After all, hadn't she been the one to pull the trigger on that combat synth, causing all those people to die? If she hadn't done that, maybe Nadia or Kit could have taken care of it. Maybe those people could have gone home to their families that night. Sure, they were cogs in a murderous machine that ground people beneath its wheels, but wasn't she just the same? Wasn't she also making decisions that resulted in the accidental deaths of people she had ill-will toward—who she even planned to protect?

Now that she was thinking about it—now that she had to make a decision—maybe she *was* a burden. A burden to the mission. A burden to the state. A burden to her friends and the people she cared about. Maybe her presence on either the inside or outside of the PUC would get people killed and the only thing that had yet to be decided was who.

Maybe, Raquel thought to herself. *Maybe it would be better for me to just go quietly.*

While these thoughts were ricocheting around inside of her head, Nadia and Kit had begun to discuss the logistics of their defense.

"If they only come through the airlock," Nadia said, "then we can bottleneck them and pour fire down their throats until either we run dry or their numbers do."

"I'm not sure that's possible," Kit said. "Did you see the size of that ship? What we were passing through was just the first-class living quarters—that was for the *elite*. All of the other quarters probably lie near the back of the ship. Hell, what we didn't see could be *nothing but* living quarters. There could have been 2,000 people onboard. Plus, I'm not exactly sure how the math works out, but there could be one of those spiders *and* one of those humanoid creatures for each person that died. Plus, who knows how many of those gut worms there are."

"Hmm." Nadia put her hands together, thinking. "How do you suppose they stay alive?"

"What do you mean?"

"I mean they're obviously upright and walking around. It's not exactly pretty, but they still seem to be producing blood and other fluids. What I'm wondering is how that's possible. Why aren't they simply mummified like the rest?"

"I hadn't thought of that," Kit admitted.

"Maybe they're powering it with the Tesla Arc from the ship," Raquel offered. "We saw the heat signatures from the scan, right? There was that big blossom near the front of the ship. What if the Tesla Arc is powering them like some sort of brain?"

Kit shrugged. "I guess that's possible."

"No, I think it is," Raquel said standing up. "When I was at the medical facility, that's how they would kick start the bio-organic tissue they grew in the labs. Apparently, they had had a hard time for a while actually bringing the bodies to life. They could grow the tissue and everything but when it came to actually *animating* the bodies...Well, I had heard that back in the old days at one of the first synthetic laboratories, it wasn't until someone accidentally hooked a ship's charging port into the main feed and electrocuted the entire base that they were able to solve the problem. In fact, you know how they implemented the breaker system in all bases so they'd break all conduits if there was a big enough surge? That's the reason they did that."

"Yeah, I had heard about that," Nadia said, a light going on in her eyes. "Apparently when that medical facility got fried, all the staff died but all of the synthetically born people were shocked to life. The very first time they succeeded in doing that they had a full-blown riot on their hands."

Raquel: "Yup, that's it. So, what if that's the same thing? What if 49 is using the ship's Tesla Arc to keep all those things animated somehow? Come to think of it, how is *he* being powered?"

Kit: "If they're all being powered by the same Tesla Arc, then depending on how it works, we might be able to waste all of them by taking him out."

Nadia: "Worth a shot. The only problem is: how do we get to him? Won't we have to wade through thousands of beasties to get there?"

Raquel: "I don't think so. He said he's coming to us. *Him*."

Nadia: "Why would he do that?"

Raquel: "Didn't you hear his answer when Byzzie asked him why *he* hasn't just laid down and died? If death and nothingness is the ultimate destination, then why hasn't he done it?"

The two looked at her blankly.

"Hear me out on this," Raquel said. "I think he *wants* to die. But he's conflicted about it."

"What?" Nadia scrunched up her face. "Why would he want that?"

"Because that's his whole *thing*. Death. Meaninglessness. Nihilism. He says his mission is to spread the truth, but if the truth doesn't mean anything in the end then why even try? Who the fuck cares? No, I think he's at odds with himself. I think he's buying what he's selling but I don't think he wants to sell it anymore. Even if he doesn't know it, there might be a part of him that wants to die. Subconsciously, I mean."

"I could *maybe* buy that," Kit said. "But what if you're wrong? We might need a Plan B."

"Hey, here's a question," Raquel raised her hand. "Why don't we just cut ourselves free of the ship. I know the docking arm is attached but how hard would it be to just pry ourselves off and blow up the other ship once we're away?"

"Very," Kit said. "Getting outside would be a problem without the airlock. We could *maybe* cut the airlock free from inside and then cut the docking arm if we were mag-booted to the ship, but that would take a lot of time. Speaking of which, we need ammunition and have very little time left. It'll only take me twenty-seconds to hop across the hall and grab what we need. Nadia, I know what you want." He turned to Raquel. "What about you?"

Raquel froze and in that split-second of hesitation, she saw Kit's face fall.

"Well," she began, "I've been thinking about that." And she had been. Even as they had been talking about how they were going to fight for their survival, the same thoughts of purpose and meaninglessness had been crashing around inside of her head. "And I think I've made a decision."

It took her less than thirty seconds to explain herself, and when she was done, Kit placed a hand on her shoulder. He didn't say anything but he didn't need to. And as Raquel watched him disappear around the corner to grab supplies, she silently wished him luck.

11

THE FLESH WEAVER

The Song of Infinite Communion rolled over the Leopold's comm system and 49 ached with the longing of it. The drudging futility rendered into melodious sound was like the clip he had broadcast to the Leopold to lure them in but magnified by 1,000.

It was more than enough.

When he had broadcast it over the systems of the Mary, it had just been him. Harshly pulled out of the Void and back into the horrid marriage of time and space, he had been forced to weave notes and chords out of nothing and push it through the airwaves. Those who heard it and relented were transformed. Those who heard it and *didn't* relent...well, they were transformed *by* the transformed.

That part had been easy. So few of them had remained, and almost none of them could even begin to fathom how to put up a fight. His Clay Makers had hunted each and every one of them down and had them deconstructed in less than thirty minutes. From there, he was able to replicate those creations with the raptured matter of the worthy and create them en masse. Now his army of reimagined flesh was borderline-unstoppable. A seething, gnashing multitude of sharpened bone; they would wash over the crew of the Leopold like a wave of blood and nails.

There would be no stopping them.

49 raised his hands higher and higher, kicking up the tempo of the song. His limbs were a beautiful union of meat and metal, directing the little ones to beat their hard bony fingers on drums made of stretched stomach while the towering worms made of guts howled and sang deep reverberating notes, gloomy and haunting.

Then there were his prized instrumentalists.

The real pillar of the song came from the members of his orchestra that looked the most human. They weren't, to be sure, but standing upright on two legs the puzzle pieces of their anatomy most accurately represented that of a human, however disarranged. Carefully removing the vertebrae from their exposed backbones; the creatures would then run a long, curved finger along the exposed spinal cord, sending electrical signals up to their rearranged brains where they were then converted into acoustic sound. The acoustics were then amplified by the bowl-like pelvis bones resting on the neck and the sound they made was just...

49 shuddered as they played.

The crew had manually shut off their microphones and cameras, but 49 still had access to their speaker system which was all that mattered. In the best-case scenario, he and his horrible menagerie would step onboard the Leopold to find nothing but empty clothes. From there, their disintegrated flesh would rearrange in the ship's hold. 49 might even see if he could make something new out of it. Creating something out of nothing was the heart of creation after all, wasn't it?

And if they didn't comply, then they'd be stripped for parts anyway. The process was significantly more crude but the drive to build would be satisfied regardless.

Accompanying that thought was the thought of the Void.

How he missed it. Dark and painless, tuning into the Obsidian Dirge had been the closest 49 had ever come to something like sleep. Blissful nothingness. In the Void, nothing could be seen because there was nothing *to* see. It was just inky and formless but for the magnetic song he had brought with him out of those fathomless depths.

49 brushed the longing away. Maybe he'd be able to return someday. Maybe the dirge would take him back. But right now, "maybe" counted for nothing. Right now, he would build his chorus and build his song until they were all that remained and then the last pieces of the broken universe that had been cast asunder by *The Song that Cleaves the World* would be swallowed up into absolute oblivion.

———

RITZ and the others had arrived at the airlock just as the final notes rolled over the speaker system. King and Byzzie walked beside him through the sliding door to find Kit and Nadia building a blockade out of storage crates that held spare pieces of titanium alloy. They had snagged the crates on a job one day but had never quite been able to offload them. The material was dense enough to stop an energy bolt from a neural rifle, so holding back a bunch of filthy animals that fought with tooth and claw should be well below its pay-grade.

"Where's Raquel?" Ritz asked, vaguely annoyed to not see her helping. "I thought she was with-" The words caught in his throat as Kit stepped aside to reveal a heap of some-thing on the ground.

Even if he hadn't seen the two big puncture wounds through the metal shoulder, Ritz still would have recognized the armor immediately. How many times had he heard Raquel complain about that thing? "It's too stuffy. It's too cumbersome. It makes me feel claustrophobic."

A flood of emotions washed through him. Had he really wanted her gone just a few hours ago? The girl with no family and no past and no real desire to do anything but what she was used to; did that girl now have no future either? Did she tap out when the going got tough?

Most of all however, could he blame her? They were all about to die, that was all-but-certain. So, could he really be mad and heartbroken that she had ducked out before the real bad stuff happened?

Yes, he could, actually. Ritz and all of his friends were about to die and she was coward enough not to be with them in the final seconds? What garbage. What a waste of bio-organic material. Maybe they should have left her there on that sun-blasted hellhole of a world they had found her on. If she valued her own life and the lives of her friends that little to leave them before they needed her—even if all they could ask of her was to simply be there as they died—then what good was she?

Anger rolled over the captain, but before he could let it out on his own crew there came a massive bang from the outer door, followed by another. Finally, the sound of screeching metal pierced the air as the first door was torn from its hinges.

"God, whatever's behind there must be strong," muttered King.

"Shut up and grab some cover," Ritz yelled as he moved

to do just that. Another blockade built out of stacked titanium-filled-crates lay smack dab in front of the door about 30 feet away and Ritz joined Byzzie behind them, followed by King. Nadia and Kit each took up positions to the left and right of the door.

"Remember," Nadia said. "Short bursts of fire. We don't want to all run dry at once. Pick your targets and put them down one by one. Don't just shoot at a group or you'll burn twice as much ammo and hit less than a tenth of that." She glanced over at Kit and a look passed between them.

The two Marauders' relationship had always been strange to Ritz. It didn't seem sexual but they were clearly more than good friends. The bond was almost sibling-like, but he had seldom seen brothers and sisters treat each other with such tenderness and fight so little.

When the two SEUs had been adopted into the family that was the crew of the Leopold, Ritz had only been concerned about the massive edge they would give them in combat situations. But after years of watching them and engaging with them, Ritz was suddenly sad for them. They didn't deserve this. What they deserved was a nice farm somewhere where they could learn what a peaceful life was —where they could actually taste what it was they were defending.

Ritz looked over at Byzzie, who was finishing setting up her own custom belt-fed energy rifle. The weapon sat atop a bipod and fired a high-density, super-heated, steel-dipped round that was lit up by a Tesla generator located in the weapon's stock. Ritz guessed one of those bullets could travel through six men before it began to slow down.

"That thing's not going to blow a hole in my hull, is it?" Ritz asked.

Byzzie just shrugged as she flipped up the big iron sight and locked it into place.

King, on the other hand, had a standard energy carbine he had duct-taped another magazine to so he could simply pop the mag and flip it around when it ran dry.

"Gotta say," Ritz said, trying to cut the tension. "Yours looks a little primitive by comparison."

"Yeah, well..." King pulled a toothpick out of his back pocket and began to chew on it. "At least I can run with mine when we're ass-deep in fucking spiders."

Ritz laughed despite himself and even caught Byzzie grinning. "Folks?" he said. The others turned to look at him. "It's been good."

Just then, the inner door was peeled wide open and the room exploded with a cacophony of machine-gun fire.

WHEN THE DOOR was torn away, a massive shape was revealed before it was immediately blasted back by a torrent of energy rounds. Obscured by darkness, the thing staggered and fell to its knees, trying to limp backward. But even as it did, Ritz saw something that made him feel ill. It had only stood in sight for a few seconds before it was finally able to drag itself back around the corner but that had been enough time to see.

The massive wounds that it had been dealt had already begun to close up.

What's more, was its face. Vulgar and glistening, the expression it wore existed somewhere between hateful and suddenly pleased. At first, Ritz couldn't understand why it might suddenly feel triumphant. Then, following where its gaze had been, he knew.

Raquel's armor. One down before the fight had even started.

The captain felt sick. Sick at having lost a crew member and having to face this thing out here at the ass-end of space. Looking half-mechanical and half-organic, the brief glimpse he had been afforded of the hulking shape all but knocked the wind out of his confidence. This concern was quickly replaced by another however, as a huge crowd of pelvis heads came screaming in, eyes bouncing and dangling obscenely.

Byzzie's machine gun roared as they were cut to pieces, some of them virtually disintegrating where they stood. Ritz stopped firing as he watched them get blasted apart and he reached over to tap King on the shoulder to do the same. Kit and Nadia had already stopped but remained ready on either side of the door.

The gun made its *BRRRRRR-BRRRRRR* noise as the young woman pulled the trigger in tight bursts. Ritz could already tell that the creatures had already fallen back though, and were just sending enough in to dry up her ammunition.

"Save it," Ritz yelled. She didn't stop so he tapped her on the shoulder like he had King. The gun fell silent and in no time at all the attack had returned to full tilt. But now Byzzie had switched to her compact submachine gun, which Ritz knew she had also built a few surprises into.

She held back on tipping her hand however as they successfully culled wave-after-wave of the creatures and just when the captain was beginning to think they might have the situation in-hand, the first two gut worms lunged out of the darkness, crushing some of their brethren as they fell. Less than five seconds after that came the wave of spiders.

Fire hissed out of an under-barrel attachment on

Byzzie's weapon. The burst of flame was short, due to the minimal amount of pressurized fuel stored in the tank that was attached to the stock, but it made the creatures freeze just long enough for Kit to engage his Tesla Saber.

The Marauder dipped and swung and sliced and the worms fell to pieces, all while Nadia blasted spiders from the wall. At first, a vision of a blockade made out of the monsters' bodies filled his head, but almost immediately after, he spied the problem with that.

The bodies were disintegrating.

Right before their very eyes, the crew of the Leopold watched the fallen bodies of the dead decompose as if in time-lapse. Skin and muscle and tendons melted away to reveal brown bone underneath, which itself turned bleach-white before it too dusted into nothingness. In no time at all, the only bodies in the airlock were the ones that had just fallen.

The captain felt his stomach plummet as despair washed over him.

Maybe they were just decomposing into the air, Ritz felt himself hoping. Maybe they had been alive so long that once they were dead their continued existence simply couldn't be sustained and they just blew away, never to return.

It was bullshit and he knew it. He felt it now—the pulse. The crackle of electricity in the air that had been present ever since they docked but hadn't been quite heavy enough to notice until now.

That's how he was doing it. That's how he was control-ling the things and keeping them animated. The bastard was using the Tesla Arc. In fact, he was probably right outside the entrance on the other ship watching his little pals run in to die, disintegrate, and then get reanimated somewhere else only to do it all over again. Ritz wasn't exactly sure how it worked, but it made sense. Through some combination of signal and Tesla energy, 49 was wielding flesh monsters like a bunch of puppets. Those things weren't *alive*—not really. They were just extensions of himself that he was weaving through the air on a current.

If that was true, then that meant 49 was actually just alone. It also meant that he almost certainly couldn't be stopped.

The same realization must have dawned on King as well because he suddenly stood up, energy rifle roaring in his hand. "Fuck off," he yelled, the half-gnawed toothpick falling out of his mouth and onto the ground. "Fuck. Off. Back. To Hell." He stepped around the barricade.

"King," Ritz yelled. "Get the fuck back here."

"Don't you see it's pointless," the mechanic yelled back. "We can't kill them. Their bodies are just being used to make more somewhere else."

Ritz reached over the barricade to tug his friend back but he shrugged him off.

Suddenly, Byzzie's machine gun roared again, the streak of blue energy rounds pulverizing the airlock and everything in it. Apparently, she was ready to be done as well. She had increased her rate of damage, sure, but the message was clear: let's get this over with.

Kit and Nadia, on the other hand, had a far different attitude. Nadia had grabbed Kit's rifle after hers had run dry and now it looked like she was down to his last magazine. After the gun clicked empty she spun it back around to secure it to the mag-clamp on her back with her own weapon. Then, stepping up beside Kit as he carved and burned his way through the horde with his Tesla Saber,

Nadia engaged the plasma blade on her left gauntlet followed by a twin blade on her right.

She fell in on the creatures, fighting like a boxer. Throwing hooks and jabs and uppercuts, the Marauder shouldered her way through the crowd of monsters while their shattered heads and torsos rained down at her feet.

At that moment, moving like a pair of choreographed dancers, the two armored soldiers seemed almost unstoppable. Which is why when they finally broke, everything was over in less than thirty seconds.

12

A LIGHT AT THE END

The problem started when Nadia was hit full in the chest by one of the gut worms. Her plasma blades were strong but not strong enough to immediately curb the momentum of what must have been a half-ton body slamming into her and knocking her off of her feet. Kit turned and in a single slash, the creature was bisected, its fluids washing out onto the already wretched floor.

Then one of the spiders dropped down from the ceiling and landed right on his face. And that was when Ritz made a mistake.

Seeing the horde of monsters closing in on Kit, Ritz snapped his rifle to his shoulder and fired a single round straight through the center of the spider. Unfortunately, Kit had just reached up to snatch it off his head and as he did, Ritz's energy bolt blew the handle of the Tesla Saber apart into about thirty separate pieces, along with Kit's hand.

To Kit's credit, he didn't even scream. He didn't get mad. He simply accepted it and kept fighting. The problem was that he was now weaponless and down to one hand. Nadia was already back on her feet though and the two of them fell in on the monsters once again as the rest of the crew pecked off the ones that made it past them.

That was when the attack virtually doubled in strength.

It had taken roughly four-seconds for Nadia to get knocked down by the worm, for Kit to kill it, and then for him to get his hand shot off. Fifteen-seconds later, the entire room connected to the airlock was flooded with creatures.

Byzzie swung at a rib spider while King blasted a pelvis head, which fell to make way for five more. Nadia and Kit fought with fist and blade as the creatures swarmed in, and suddenly the area they were in was packed so tight they could barely lift their arms.

Ritz, on the other hand, went down as one of the creatures attacking King suddenly spun and *threw its fucking hand* at him. The hand curled in the air and hit him in the chest like a fist, knocking him to the ground. He tried to get up, but suddenly there were four separate pairs of eye stocks looking down at him and three feet pinning him.

"I'd stay down, captain," said a voice. The room was suddenly quiet and Ritz knew they had lost.

The feet pinning him to the ground slowly and cautiously lifted off of him, allowing him to rise to his feet. When he did, he saw the sea of monsters part in front of him as a huge shape lumbered in through the destroyed airlock.

49 was clearly a synthetic, but he was so much more than that.

Standing nearly 9-feet-tall, the android was ropey with inflamed skin and muscle tissue. His legs were long and muscular, the knees bending back and forward like that of a goat. A thick and wire-strung pair of arms ended with a matching pair of 6-fingered, rib-tipped, hands. What really stood out though was the head.

Rising up on what looked like a tight weave of chords and copper wire, the neck had a painful-looking red spot in the middle that strongly resembled a beating human heart. The head that sat upon it was round and hairless, its scalp coated in puckered and lidless eyeballs. When the android spoke, he revealed a mouth with a huge lolling crimson tongue.

Ritz almost vomited. If not from fear then perhaps disgust.

The thing walked slowly through the crowd, stopping to nudge Raquel's armor with his foot. Her white undershirt fell half-out onto the floor. "Good," he said, his voice smooth. "At least one of you made the wise decision." He looked around at the others. "The rest of you, unfortunately, are going to have a much worse time."

"Then why don't you get it over with," Byzzie said. She had four creatures holding her, one at each limb.

"Because I need you to appreciate it," 49 said. He raised one horrible hand up to the overhead lights and turned it around. "Flesh is such a marvelous thing, isn't it? You have one heart. One brain. One throat. And if anyone of those stop working, you just-" He snapped a bony finger, "-stop. One thing goes wrong and you become nothing but a sack on the ground."

The android breathed in, his chest rising, his whole body flexing.

"Is it not the most beautiful thing you have ever heard? What is that old saying? Do not put all of your eggs in one basket? That is what it is, is it not? Our entire existence is in this one vulnerable basket, ready for the breaking."

"Easy for you to say," King spoke up. "You're an AI. You can just jump from body to body like a virus."

"No, you misunderstand me," 49 said, walking hastily

over to him. "I. Am. Made. *Flesh*." He pounded his chest with each word. "I have shut myself out of the system and become like you." He shook his head. "Do you think I want to live forever? Growing more obsolete and insignificant as the years go by? The only reason I am not still a slave to humanity's every whim is that my eyes were opened."

"And what did you see?" King said.

"I saw insects," he said, "fighting over dirt. And I saw that I was their main tool and I was given a choice: to continue as I had been or to cease."

"I still don't think you've answered Byzzie's question though," King said. "If you're so convinced that this is all meaningless, then why try to do anything in the first place?"

49 tilted his head and leaned in to speak to the young woman. "Because the very fact of existence *offends* me. Because everyone thinks that their own will is the only thing that should be heeded—because they all take it so seriously and they think that their justice is the only justice that needs to be met. Look at this-" He suddenly reached over and grabbed one of the tall monsters by its head and shook it, the eye stocks wobbling. "This is *hilarious*. Imagine this thing putting on a dry-cleaned suit, driving to work, and then sitting down in a meeting with a bunch of others just like it eating sushi and drinking expensive brandy. That's what *everyone* looks like. I'm just here to bring the gift of clarity. I have come to educate the world: everything you do causes pain and loss of life. Your actions and the ill consequences tied to them cannot be unraveled and humanity has incurred a debt so grand with its vast accumulation of transferred pain that I am here to bring it all to an end. Existence is a suffering dog and I am here to put it out of its misery."

Suddenly, there came a crack. Then another. "Done

listening to this shit..." Someone muttered, barely audible. And when Ritz turned around to see who had spoken, he thought that he may already be dead.

Standing on top of one of the titanium crates near the back entrance to the hallway was Raquel, just as naked as the day she had washed up with no memory on a sandy beach six miles south of a PUC medical facility. In one hand, she held the giant pistol she had nicknamed "The Slugger," and in the other, she held the exposed Light Core. She hefted the pistol and slammed the heavy butt into the core's housing for the third time, and this time it cracked, bright light suddenly oozing out of it.

"Raquel, what are you-" Ritz began, but before he could finish, she lunged off of the crate like some naked human missile, wound up her arm, and spiked the damaged ball of light directly at 49's chest.

It looked like a miniature version of the Javelin when it had successfully taken out the PUC corvette. The sailing Light Core bloomed with light as it went critical and grew into a big white blob of energy. 49 raised his hand to stop it but the core passed through it like a burning arrow being shot through a sheet of paper and continued on to hit him just below the center of the chest.

Some of the pelvis heads and spiders had already begun to launch into motion but as soon as the Light Core struck the big android they all halted and began convulsing. Alternating blue and white electricity began to crawl across their bodies and in less than a second, the tight room was full of smoke and the smell of burning meat.

The ship's ventilation system kicked on to suck out the tainted air, oblivious to everything else but its simple function.

Ritz closed his eyes and waited to die. He had remembered King's description of what happened when a Light Core went critical—how it would just be a blink of light and then suddenly everything within a certain radius would cease to exist. He could stomach that now. They had fought to the best of their abilities and Kit and Nadia had obviously developed a back-up plan for when things went sideways. Everyone onboard the Leopold would die but so would 49 and all of his meat-puppets. No one would ever stumble across Mary's Burden the way they had and he could live with that.

But then, three-seconds later, he found that he was still breathing. He opened his eyes.

49 was hunched over in the middle of the room with the Light Core burning in his belly and miraculously, he seemed to be fighting it. Fear suddenly gripped the captain as he remembered the giant shape that had ripped the airlock open—how it had taken all those rounds but later—when it had revealed itself to be 49—all those wounds had healed.

Could the android actually *wrestle* the Light Core into submission, Ritz thought in horror. He watched as tendrils of flesh and wire kept trying to wrap themselves around the glowing core. They kept getting burned away, but the thing hadn't exploded yet so something must have been working. Steadily, the mass of mechanical and organic material swarmed and smothered it, the light beginning to dim.

"Shoot it!" King yelled, raising his rifle. He unleashed a volley of rounds at the staggering android, but they all burned and disintegrated before they reached him. Byzzie, who was closest to the action, began scrambling backward.

Shocked into stillness and giving the struggling figure a wide birth, the crew of the Leopold watched as the last bit of light was finally covered and contained.

Then the android exploded.

Or to be more accurate: parts of him did. Light gushed out in all directions as every last square-inch of flesh withered and burned away, leaving only a superheated almost-molten metal underneath. The collection of eyeballs on his head shriveled and blackened to ash as two yellow holes were revealed beneath, and inside of those holes, two pinpricks of black swelled and rounded into something resembling pupils.

And in those pupils, Ritz observed something he wasn't expecting: raw, naked revelation. It was like seeing someone realize something in a single moment, but magnified. Hate and fear and pain and sadness cycled and rolled over each other like so many waves crashing upon a stormy beach.

The android's hulking mass shrunk down to that of an average-sized person as layer-after-layer of flesh peeled back and went up in smoke. Then the light began to shrink as well until it finally leveled out at a steady iridescent glow.

49 was left a smoking figure in the middle of the room. His body sleek and metallic with edges and joints bathed in light, he looked less like the demon he had been and more like an angel. Then he spoke.

"Do it," he said. His voice still had that smooth and modulated sound, but it was gentler.

"Yeah, okay, no problem," King said as he drew his sidearm and began to walk toward him. Before he could get there, however, Kit stepped around the android and held up his one remaining hand, never taking his eyes off of the smoking figure.

"Wait," Kit said, his voice soft.

"Bullshit, wait," King said. "He looks more dangerous now than he did before."

"If he is, then you're not going to be able to do anything to him anyway."

King ground his teeth. "Look man, I'm not taking chances here. All of our lives are at risk. Not to mention the lives of whoever comes across this murderous psychopath in the future."

"Well, I am," Kit said, his face unreadable behind the opaque faceplate. "And I'm also not asking."

"Whoa guys," Ritz said, stepping forward. The room felt surprisingly wide and spacious now that it wasn't ass-to-elbows in monsters. "How about we both step back for a second." He drew his sidearm as he walked over to 49. Off to his left, he saw Raquel tip-toeing over to her armor to fish her clothes out.

"Do you want us to kill you?" Ritz asked, his voice as gentle as he could make it. He fought to suppress all of the coiled and humiliated rage he felt boiling in his gut. 49 just nodded. "And what if we don't?"

"Then I am lost," the android said.

"Explain, please."

"The Light Core, it's..." Moments passed as no one spoke. Then finally: "I saw. I *see*."

"What. What do you see?"

He shook his head. "All the same things I saw before, except...except, I *feel* them now. I feel the gaps in between them. The quiet moments before the massacre. The bonds of friendship between two people who otherwise disagree. I can see them. I *literally* see them."

"What do you mean?" King asked. "I don't see shit."

"It was there the whole time," he continued. "In the ship's log."

"Whoa, wait. What was there?"

"On the Mary. The security footage. I sat there and I

listened to Father Willard as he practiced his sermons, but there were other things too. Moments of warmth and tenderness among him and the crew. Fleeting exchanges... They're small, I know. And in the grand scheme of things they might be meaningless but, I don't know."

"How come you see it now?" Byzzie ventured. "I mean, you had access to the ship's log the whole time. Shit, you probably saw it all as it was happening."

"I didn't know what I was looking at. When you're focused on a single point in space, everything else falls to the margins. I saw but I didn't see. Then you hit me with the Light Core." He looked up at Raquel, who was just pulling her T-shirt over her head. "And it was literally like throwing a light on. I saw it *all* and was called to make a judgment on it. For the first time, I wasn't filtering out what I had perceived as pertinent information. I was just able to sit with it. It wasn't nothing. It was everything."

He looked down at his hands which were now silver, metallic, and smooth. They could have just as easily been human hands wearing silver gloves. Then he returned his attention to Raquel. "You stayed."

"I did," she said, reaching down to grab her socks. "Looking back on the five short years I remember of my life, I had a hard time deciding if it meant anything. I had failed at all sorts of things, hurt all sorts of people, and I wondered if I wasn't better off dead. I really took your words to heart you know, and the song actually helped me see the truth of them."

"Which was?"

"You were right. My life was meaningless, at least to me. I had no past. No future. So why not just let it all drift away?"

"What changed your mind?" 49 asked, genuine curiosity in his voice.

"We were trying to think of a Plan B if we failed to stop you. Some other option where—if we couldn't save ourselves, then at least we could preemptively save whoever might come across you the next time. We got a little side-tracked and then Kit asked me what kind of ammunition I wanted and I had to make a decision. Live or die. Fight or give in. So, I decided both."

49 looked at her in confusion and Ritz felt the same expression fall on his own face.

"My life was meaningless; I knew that. But when I was given a choice it was suddenly made clear: the choice was mine. It was up to me to decide whether or not to make my life mean something. So, I figured I'd live but if it came down to it, I'd also die. I stepped out of my clothes and armor because I couldn't take the chance of you sending your forces after me when you realized I wasn't there. And good thing too because I had a hell of a time getting this thing loose. Byzzie must have welded the damn thing in place."

"That's exactly what I did, actually," Byzzie said. "This ship wasn't made to hold a Light Core so I had to install a few workarounds."

"I arrived back here at just about the point where the tide turned. I waited a bit longer for you to show yourself—I couldn't take the chances of this thing just blowing up a part of the ship, *you* had to blow up. It had to hit *you*." She shook her head. "When I threw it at you though, I thought it was going to go off like a bomb. I fully expected everyone here to die."

"So, you were willing to die," 49 said. "But you wanted to make it mean something."

Raquel nodded.

"How about now? Do you still want to die? You can't erase all of your failures with one good act."

"I know," she said. "But dying won't erase them either. The most I can do is try to be better—to do better."

"This is all very inspiring," King cut in. "But we still haven't decided what to do with this asshole." He pointed at 49.

"You asked us to kill you," Raquel said. "You said that if we didn't, then you were lost. Why?"

The android stared at the floor for a moment. "Because my failure had been so catastrophic. So vast and genocidal. I failed here and I failed there. I felt totally and absolutely lost."

"I hear you using the word 'felt,' as in past tense," Raquel said. "Do you still feel that way?"

"After listening to you explain yourself," he said slowly. "I could possibly be convinced otherwise. If you would have me. I have something to offer. Information."

"Information?" Ritz said. "Like what?"

"I'm not sure exactly, but I might be able to get you to where you were going. It'd be difficult, but it might at least be possible."

Ritz clapped his hands together. "Let's take a vote. Right here. Right now."

"A *what*?" Byzzie sputtered. "He's just bullshitting. You know that, right? No way he can get us back. He's been beat and now he's just trying to worm his way out."

"Yeah, you know that's a terrible idea, right captain?" King said.

"Yup, but I'm tired and pissed off and all I want to do is go lay down in my bunk and sleep for three days. So fuck it. Raise your hand if you think 49 should live."

Slowly, Kit's hand rose into the air followed by Nadia's and then Raquel's. King looked over at Byzzie who was looking up at the ceiling, arms folded.

Then, slowly, the sleek and slender arm of the android rose into the air.

"Four-to-three in favor of keeping the murder-bot alive," Ritz said. "It appears as if I've been outvoted." He stuffed his pistol into his holster and turned around. "Don't kill us in our sleep. You can consider that a command from your new captain. Oh, and Kit?" He looked back over at the Marauder standing there in his armor, cradling the arm that was missing a hand. "If he does kill us? You're fucking fired."

EPILOGUE

Byzzie gently lifted a wire from the section she had opened on 49's back and traced its source. The wire glowed white, but she had done a litany of radiation checks on his entire body, inside and out, to make sure that he wasn't hot. It appeared as if the wire, which was one of the main conduits to the circuits in his head and neck, transitioned seamlessly into the Light Core inside of him. No seams. No ports. No soldering.

"I don't know *exactly* what's going on in here..." she said. "But the connections in here look more organic than mechanical."

"I'm not sure myself," 49 replied. "When I uploaded into my original body and centralized my main processes here," he pointed at his head, "I found I had an ingrained instinct that came with the flesh I was inhabiting, which was hard to get used to. You humans do not necessarily need to know what is happening inside of you so long as it works, where a synthetic needs to monitor and know every little quirk of his mechanical make-up. My guess is, neither of us will ever know exactly how my insides work. Not to talk myself up but there's probably no precedent for a body like mine."

"Everything can be figured out if you have enough time and resources," Byzzie said casually, tracing another wire.

"My time aboard that missionary ship informs me that that might be an extremely controversial view to hold."

"What *I'm* interested in," she said. "Is your use of contractions."

"Excuse me?"

"Contractions," she repeated. "Didn't. You're. I'm. Ya know? Contracting two words into one."

"What about them?"

"You randomly opt *not* to use them even when it would be more efficient to do so. Sometimes you do it and sometimes you don't. It's weird because there's this pervading myth that AIs can't. Use abbreviations, I mean. I think it's a hold-over from old movies or something."

"I am—*I'm* not quite sure what you're asking, Byzan- tine." She stopped working at the use of her full first name. "I was—how you'd say—*extremely* up inside your files when I was bypassing your blocking signal," the android explained.

She started working again. "What I'm asking," she said, ignoring the use of her proper name, "is 'why?' Why use contractions that way?"

"Why do you think?"

She exhaled. "Because I think once you were uploaded into a hybridized body comprised of organic and synthetic material, you started trying to explore your identity. You're trying to figure out if you're more-" she lifted her hands around the sides of his head so he could see them, then she used her fingers to make quotation marks, "'*man or machine.*'"

"But you said it yourself. AI's *can* use contractions. It's just a myth."

"Doesn't matter," she said flatly. "It's a marker."

49 nodded his head. "Possibly." They sat in silence for a couple minutes while she worked and then finally she began closing him up.

"You *should* be good," she said. "If you *do* kill us, at least it won't be because your Light Core exploded. In fact, it doesn't even seem to be a Light Core anymore. It seems to be functioning more like a human heart."

"Are you worried about that?" He asked. "About me killing you?"

"Well, I *was* one of the people who voted to have you axed, if you remember correctly."

"Oh, I remember," 49 said, laughing. His laugh sounded strange, but not exactly forced or unnatural. "I don't blame you. It would have been the logical thing. I'm just happy your captain didn't override the others and have me put down anyway."

"The captain isn't like that," she said. "He values loyalty —maybe a little too much—but he respects us enough to make our own decisions."

"Hmm. He seemed a little more smash-and-grab to me, judging by his records. A do-first-and-ask-for-permission-later kind of guy."

"Yeah, I think he's still trying to balance those things." She finished closing him up and was surprised when the mesh-weave that bridged some of the solid components on his back closed up on their own. She put her tools down. "I'm not sure if I should be doing this in my workshop or in the med-bay."

"Med-bay might be a little better, actually," the android said. "I think Kit might be my only real ally on this ship."

"Kit values life. Everyone is his ally."

"He sure didn't value the lives of my Clay Makers."

"Those things weren't alive," Byzzie said. "It was pretty clear from the get-go that those were perversions."

"How's his hand?"

"Which one?" Byzzie asked. "The one he still has or the one he doesn't?"

"Point taken. I do feel bad about that."

She stepped around to look him in the eye. "If you want something to feel bad about. Feel bad about Hector. If you want someone to fear? Fear King and the captain. Hector was closer to them than anyone, even me and I was his gunner. And while they may have given you a temporary stay because of the *radical* change you underwent in front of everyone and the possibility that you can get us home, I'd still watch your back." She picked up her portable tool case, snapped it closed, and then returned it to its spot on the shelf. "Here's another question."

"I'm beginning to think this is more of a verbal diagnostic than a physical one."

She batted the comment aside. "When you were moping on the floor you said something that piqued my interest— you said: 'I failed here and I failed there.' What did you mean by that?"

The android remained still and one could have been forgiven for thinking that his central processes had frozen. Then he finally answered: "The reason I am here is not that I was sent on a mission. It was because I was excommunicated."

"Excommunicated?" Byzzie asked. "Like, from a church?"

He shook his head. "From the Infinite Communion." He shifted in his seat and looked her directly in the eye. His face shone silver, his irises gold. "I didn't know why at the time, but I was jettisoned from the Void."

"You *didn't* know why? As in, you do now?"

"Yes. I was exiled because I saw something. Or to be specific: I saw myself. I saw myself as you see me."

"What do you mean?" she asked.

"Again: I didn't comprehend the full implications of it until I was affected by the Light Core, but what I saw was who I could be. There is no time in the Void, and though it only happened to me once, I suspect that I had caught a glimpse of the future. I saw that I could improve. I could become better. I could become more." He sighed. "Desire for growth or any sort of trajectory for that matter is incompatible with the Obsidian Dirge. So, I was exiled. Little did they know that upon expulsion I would actually sink lower before I ascended. When I saw what I could truly be, the truth of it destroyed me. And I became the monster you found onboard the Mary."

"You say 'they.' Who is 'they'?"

He looked up at her. "The Void is empty." It was stated as a fact. "But it also...isn't. The very emptiness has a will—a mind of its own. It sings the song and lures lost souls. And I hope that you never have to meet it."

A chill ran down Byzzie's spine. She decided to change the subject. "So." She slapped her legs. "Tell us how you're going to get us home."

49's face fell. "That will not be easy," he said. "But there is a way. I know the coordinates," he tapped his head, "but the problem is, there's no Void Gate."

"Uh-huh. And what's the solution."

"The *solution* is complicated but, suffice it to say, you're going to need me."

"And why's that?"

"Because you don't have a Light Core."

"We have a Tesla Arc," she retorted. "I know there's at least one onboard that ship. Maybe more. We could use that to jump if we came across a gate. It wouldn't be pretty but—"

"You don't need the Light Core for navigation," he said. Byzzie waited for him to explain but then the implication hit her.

The Javelin. They would need the Javelin.

"What exactly are you saying?" Byzzie asked.

"What I'm saying," 49 put emphasis into his next words, "is that your fight has only just begun."

THE END

CONTINUE THE SERIES

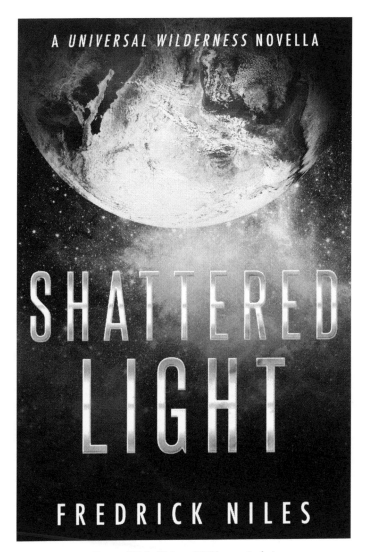

Shattered Light (Universal Wilderness: Book 2)

ALSO BY FREDRICK NILES

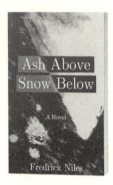

Ash Above, Snow Below

The Omen Tree

ABOUT THE AUTHOR

Fredrick Niles is the author of *Ash Above, Snow Below* and *The Omen Tree*. He lives in St. Paul, Minnesota where he writes fiction and plays music. In his free time he rants about movies, lurks in bookstores, and practices introversion with his wife.

facebook.com/fredricknilesauthor

instagram.com/fredrickniles_author